ENTERTAINING
Murder

———— ◆ ————

Mia Tenroc

ENTERTAINING MURDER by Mia Tenroc
© 2016 Mia Tenroc.
ISBN: 978-1-944433-01-7 (paperback)

McToner Publishing Inc.
P.O. Box 37
Goldenrod, Florida 32722
McTonerPublishing@gmail.com
www.Miatenroc.com

Permissions:

© Connie Larsen | Dreamstime.com
© Jrtmedia | Dreamstime.com
Cover & Formatting by Perry Elisabeth Design | perryelisabethdesign.com

DEDICATION

This book is dedicated to the ladies at my water aerobics classes. I want to thank them for all their interesting stories which are a true source of inspiration for my books.

ACKNOWLEDGMENTS

I would like to add a special thank you to Connie, Patricia, Penny, Gloria, Betty and Eric who review my books and help keep me on the right direction. I thank you for encourage me to follow my dreams of writing and for letting me share some of our life adventures.

Cast of Characters

Group of Friends:

Jean – A murder mystery writer who had involvement with murders in the past and tells the stories of her adventures to her friends. She dates police detective Nick Noble.

Josephine, aka Jo – Jean's sister, a vegetarian and animal lover who is into gardening and holistic medicine. She is married to Michael.

Francesca Anne, goes by Fannie Annie – Jean's lifelong friend. She is an eccentric bohemian that runs a secondhand shop. She loves to make herself the talk of the town.

Belinda – The optimistic, outgoing one of the group. She retired from a high-power marketing career. She and her family are well connected in high society circles. She is married to Steve.

Priscilla – Jean's next door neighbor and friend. She is the quiet person of the group that prefers to listen rather than talk. She is close to her daughter, Kathy, and two grandsons, Jerry and Craig, that live in town.

Eve – An accountant that works from home part-time. She lives next door to Josephine. Eve hates frogs. Her husband is Nigel.

Alan – Jean's son. He runs a hugely popular comic book and gaming store. He supports his mom in her investigations.

Key people related to the first murder:

Kathy ReSol – Priscilla's daughter. She was a successful business woman until a boating accident left her disabled. She has two sons, Jerry and Craig, from her marriage with Richard.

Richard ReSol – Kathy's husband. He is a dancing instructor but prefers to live off of other people's money rather than work.

Patty, aka Princess P – A sheltered, naïve heiress with a large trust fund. She becomes Richard's girlfriend after being seduced by his charm.

Charles ReSol – His only son is Richard, whom he loves dearly. He was a prosperous inventor until his health started to slowly decline due to dementia.

Helen ReSol – Charles' wife and Richard's step-mother. She married Charles for his money and hates her stepson (not that she likes anyone else anyways).

Alan and Barb – Patty's grandparents. They became Patty's guardians after her parents died. So fearful of losing Patty, they overly protected her from the outside world.

Key people related to the second murder:

Nick Noble – Jean's significant other. He is the police detective assigned to the community theatre murder.

Janice Hoover – Nick's long-time partner on the force. Her determined and sometimes fiery approach offsets Nick's laid-back demeanor.

Judith Lane – She was a part-time staff member of the community theatre. She was a quiet and sweet person who was alone in life.

Miriam Highland – The director of the community theatre group who achieved her position by sleeping with the right people. She clearly possesses a superiority complex.

Mr. Creighton – An extremely wealthy man who created the theatre company to please Miriam.

Chapter 1 – The Morning After

"I HATE HIM! I WISH HE WAS DEAD!" Those words were being shouted by Priscilla, who never raised her voice or said anything negative.

Jean's eyes opened wide quickly in shock. She had been sound asleep in the apartment next door. Normally you never heard anything between the two apartments due to the dense walls being almost soundproof. In fact, Jean hadn't heard a phone ring so she wondered if Priscilla was alone. She was getting up when she heard the door shut, the lock turn and Priscilla walking quickly downstairs.

Nick, Jean's significant other, was leaning on his elbow, "She is gone, so you might as well stay in bed. We got in very late last night and I need more sleep."

Jean began her argument, "I need to check on her to see if she's ok." Jean was dedicated to her friends and family, and disliked when they felt hurt or upset.

As he laid back on the bed, Nick countered with, "If she needed your help, she would have come over and knocked on the door. Come on and sleep some more."

Jean was not to be deterred, "She wouldn't come to the door because she knows I'm asleep and she wouldn't want to disturb me. Maybe I should call her." The phone rang but was sent to voicemail. Since she knew Priscilla was ok, Jean returned to bed.

Jean was lying with her head facing away from Nick. She was lying very still and quiet but could not sleep. Nick was a full time police detective and she knew his weekends to rest and enjoy life were very important. Finally Nick said, "We might as well get up. You're not going to get any more sleep, I can tell."

Jean turned over looking him in the eyes, "I wasn't making a sound or moving."

Nick said with a yawn, "Yes, but I can tell your blood is racing and you're about to explode so we might as well have breakfast and talk this out."

Jean snuggled close to Nick and said, "We can talk this out right here if you like." Nick placed a kiss on Jean's head as she continued, "We both know who Priscilla hated, that lousy cheating son-in-law. What if she finds out I know about it and didn't tell her?"

Nick let out a sigh, "You only had your suspicions aroused last night, and you have no proof that Richard was cheating on Kathy."

Jean rolled her eyes, "Please don't give me that. We both know he is cheating. I agree since we didn't find out until Priscilla was already in bed, I couldn't wake her to tell her what I suspected, so she should forgive me for not saying anything."

Nick was getting amused, "We don't know that he is cheating and we shouldn't tell stories without proof."

Jean laughed, "I bet we will know soon enough that he is a cheat." Jean gazed upon the great guy next to her and appreciated his logical mind versus her gut instinct. "You're right, there's nothing we can do now so let's not get up." She gave him a romantic kiss and held him close.

Nick fell back to sleep. They hadn't gotten to bed until 2:00 a.m. after he had a long day at work. Jean's mind was rethinking all that happened the night before. Nick and Jean loved to ballroom dance together. On Friday nights, the different ballrooms in the area alternated hosting an open dance It was so much fun with the dancing, visiting with old friends and enjoying the good food being served. When they entered the room, Jean immediately spotted Richard ReSol, Priscilla's son-in-law. He wanted his first name pronounced *Ri-chard* to sound French. He may have descended from a French background many generations ago, but no one in his family spoke the language or had ever set foot in France. By Richard's side, there had been a very plain, mousy-looking young woman. Even from a distance, the flirtation was obvious. As they danced, he would pull the girl close and smile as he looked deep into her eyes. She was so excited for the attention and returned the gestures. Nick and Jean actually were there for a long time, dancing and enjoying the snacks, before Richard spotted her. Jean didn't look directly at Richard, but out of the corner of her eye she saw him curse and told the girl something negative about the old woman across the room. Reading lips and reading upside down are two good skills to have in life. The girl didn't even try to be sneaky as she turned to look at Jean. Richard grabbed the girl's hand and was walking to the door when he looked back. Jean was staring straight at him with a slight smile on her lips but anger in her eyes.

Richard smiled and waved. He brought the girl over while turning on his charm with Jean. "It is good to see you, Jean. We were just about to leave when I saw you. After all, this is a dance lesson and I have to get home soon. This is Patty, one of my dance students. It's one thing to learn in the classroom with no one else around and another to mingle with the other dancers trying not to run into anyone. Patty is going to her cousin's wedding in a couple of weeks and wanted a more real life experience, so I suggested the lesson be here tonight. I do hope you are having fun at this venue, since as an instructor at this location, I feel the need to also be a host."

The whole time Richard was talking, he was smiling and acting very open about his presence with another woman. Jean carried her end of the conversation in a pleasant manner inquiring about the wedding details and the length of time Patty had been taking dancing lessons. Patty seemed to like to talk to anyone that would listen to her so she went on in great detail while Richard shifted from one foot to another. When the couple finally made their escape, Jean had to wrestle with the decision about what to say and how much to tell Priscilla and her daughter. Nick warned Jean then, as he did now, that they didn't have any proof or facts that cheating was actually going on. Nick thought it was best not to say anything but if Jean did causally mention seeing Richard, she should only repeat what he told her, that he was working with a student. Only tell the facts you know and nothing more was Nick's motto.

Nick was sleeping soundly with a smooth rhythm to his breathing, and before she even knew it, Jean was asleep too.

Chapter 2 – Saturday's Lunch

Nick and Jean awoke about 10:30 a.m., showered, dressed and left the apartment, going to Josephine and Michael's house for lunch. Family and friends shorten Josephine's name to Jo. Normally they would meet Jo, Jean's sister, and her husband Michael at the diner because of the differences between Jo and Nick on their taste of food. Josephine was a vegetarian that liked lightly sautéed vegetables, and Nick preferred meat with his meals and vegetables well done. Josephine did have an incredible talent for gardening and also had a greenhouse so she had fresh foods all year long. A crop of beans and corn was ready so with Jo agreeing to cook them to a soft stage, Nick compromised on no meat. After all, dinner wasn't that far away.

The little village of Abeltown where they lived was built on a grid pattern with six streets running north or south with traditional old town names and six streets running east and west with numbers as names. The town was so small that no one drove unless they were leaving it. Today, Nick and Jean walked taking the first right, going south one block before turning left onto Third Street. On the corner was the church where Nick and Jean had exchanged vows. They both reached to hold hands when they neared the church. The happy couple met a number of years ago. Both have grown families, both had been divorced and both were leery of a second try. Both had strong religious beliefs and didn't feel right being together without a commitment. Like so many older couples, they also stood to lose financial benefits if they got married so the solution was to get morally married but not legally. They wrote and exchanged vows to each other in church. They were committed to one another. All the family and friends understood and respected the couple as unified. There were many jokes about being halfway there and being almost a part of the family, but as long as they felt good about it, that was the important part.

Nick was still an active police detective that worked in a large city that was about 10 miles away. He looked about 10 years younger than his age with no body fat and rock hard abs. Nick was very good looking, being tall with blonde hair and blue eyes. Jean was a few years older and worked hard at staying fit but was a little heavy by nature.

Luckily, Jean looked about 15 years younger than her age since she was a little older than Nick. Jean took an early retirement from her 9 to 5 job when she became successful writing murder mysteries. She was originally from Abletown and loved it there. While she still owned a house in the city, she found the quiet town a better place to write, so she moved back and took a room at a senior's home that her grandfather helped to build about 100 years before. Most people didn't want to live in a home that old and it wasn't really easy for someone with back or hip problems, so most people preferred to live in a modern house on Sixth Street or in the larger city. Jean liked the peace and quiet of small town living. Nick was often working late and odd hours so living apart eased the obligation of adjusting their hours to suit the other's lifestyle.

Jo and Michael lived in an older two story home about four blocks down. Most houses in town sat only a couple of steps from the sidewalk but had a larger back yard. There was a nice large screened porch across the back of the house in which Jo had set up the table for their meal. As they sat, Jo said, "I thought Priscilla might come with you. I made a fruit salad that she is very fond of, so why don't you take some home?"

"I didn't realize you invited her," said Jean.

Josephine explained, "I didn't really, but sometimes she comes since she is always welcome. Didn't she see you leave?"

Jean replied carefully, "I heard her up and leaving the apartment early today. I'm not sure where she was going because she didn't say anything last night about having plans today, but being Saturday we don't stick to our usual routine. I noticed her car was gone when we left so I will probably see her later. I will be glad to give her the food." Nick liked that Jean did not gossip and spread false rumors.

The conversation changed to planning the dedication of the old graveyard in town. The site was across from the Hicksite Church and next to the Orthodox Church.

Nick said, "Who knew there were two types of Quakers?"

Jean quickly corrected him, "Technically, they call themselves the Society of Friends, not Quakers."

The two-hundred-year-old cemetery was on roughly three city lots. The markers were all gone so the sisters were researching who was buried there. After getting permission from any descendants, they planned to get new markers, the design being small flat white granite with the names in bronze. The sisters then planned to surround the area with a white picket fence, all at their own expense. They had been researching the residents of the graveyard and had a small story about each person buried there and their contribution to the growth of the town. Today, Abletown had about 1,500 residents, the largest ever in the history of the town. The growth was due to city dwellers discovering the charm of a small town and yet being close enough to enjoy the cultural activities and events in the city.

Lunch was just ending when Jo brought out a cherry pie. Jean appreciated the dessert choice because she was trying to avoid extra calories and since her sister knew Jean disliked fruit pies, she didn't need to make an excuse to refuse. Jo was actually being kind to her sister by not fixing something sweet that would tempt her. They saw another friend of theirs walking to her house two doors away and waved.

Chapter 3 – Frogs

Eve had a way of creating comedy and drama at the same time which created a story a day for the others to talk about. Eve was happily married because her husband, Nigel, lived in a junkyard outside of town. He called it a collection of treasures, but to Eve it was junk. It was the type of place a picker longed to see. They had lived together about 15 years in the city until the Code Enforcement Board threatened that either he got rid of the junk or he would face stiff penalties and maybe even community service time. Unable to part from his "stuff," Eve bought an old farm in the country and moved him and all his possessions to a place in which it was acceptable to live in disarray. Eve always hated the junk and was so glad to have a nice clean home. Eve had a daughter from a previous marriage and a granddaughter that kept moving in and out of their home, and it was a source of irritation for

Nigel. To pay for the farm, Eve sold their big house with lots of land which left just enough money to buy the little house in Abletown for herself. The location was 15 minutes to Eve's job on the edge of the city and 20 minutes the opposite way to see her husband. Eve hoped the small house would deter her family from moving in with her.

The house was two bedrooms, one bath, and a small front room with a large fireplace on one wall. There was a screened porch off the kitchen. When the granddaughter, Linda, moved in, Eve, who usually worked from home, was forced to move her office to the porch. Eve's clothes that had filled the closet of the spare bedroom were put on a metal rack and the shoes in boxes, adding to the clutter on the porch. Eve then covered the screens with thick plastic to keep the weather from getting on the items when it rained.

Linda's friend had an above ground pool for sale that she agreed to purchase if he would set it up for her in the backyard. Eve was very angry about it because Linda didn't do any work around the house and a pool is a lot of work to take care of. Eve told Linda that it was her responsibility to clean the pool. The pool ended up looking like a mucky swamp and was loaded with wildlife, including tadpoles that grew into loud frogs which Eve hated.

Eve walked through the house putting her purse on the kitchen table as she carried file folders with this week's receipts to the porch to begin her work. A blood curdling scream came from the porch causing Michael, Nick, Jo and Jean to come running.

"What's wrong?" shouted Josephine.

Sobbing and unable to move, Eve was pointing to the floor of the porch. She was surrounded with what looked like a hundred frogs. "HELP! Get them out of here!"

It appears that Linda left the back door to the porch open when she went out to her car to leave that day. Jo pushed Eve into the house, "The three of you need to get the frogs out of here without hurting them."

Jean found a large empty cardboard box and the three kept lifting the lid and stuffing in frog after frog.

Eve, while crying, grabbed her phone, "What's the number for animal control?"

Jo tried to take the phone from Eve's hand, "Calm down. This isn't a matter for animal control. The problem is being solved." Jo, looking out of the window of the door shouted, "Hurry and get them all out of here but be careful not to step on any. Don't hurt them by squeezing too hard."

These comments were answered by dirty looks from the three workers. Jean turned her back to her sister and started laughing, "This really is funny. You can expect this to appear in a book someday. Both of them are acting like fools."

It took about an hour before those on frog patrol felt they had them all but Eve could not be calmed so Jo gathered the laptop, files, packed a suitcase for the night and took Eve home. "A nice cup of herbal tea will calm you."

Michael volunteered, "I will take the frogs far away. There is a good place to put them in the stream which is miles from the house. I will stay in the area and make sure the relocation goes smoothly."

Jo said, "Thank you so much. I will feel so much better knowing they are in a good home."

Michael told Nick and Jean in a voice that only they could hear, "I plan to watch them from the pub on the boat dock for a long time. I'm sure it will take hours for the adjustment. That's with the hope of Eve being over her crying and Jo being over her worrying for the frog's safety."

Nick laughed, "Sounds like a sensible plan to me."

Nick and Jean headed back to the apartment walking up Third Street, turning right onto Main which took them past Fannie Annie's Attic, owned and operated by another friend of Jean's when the next event of the day occurred.

Chapter 4 – Fannie's Logic

Fannie, whose real name was Francesca Anne, yelled from the door of the antique and consignment shop, "Will you get in here now and help me get this man's pants on?!"

Nick turned to Jean with hands on his hips, "You have the most unusual friends."

"Come on, I'm in a hurry", shouted Fannie. Unsure what to expect, Nick and Jean entered the shop. On the floor was a male mannequin without any clothes on. Jean was grateful it wasn't anatomically correct; in fact the section of the mannequin below the waist and above the legs was missing. There were boxes of clothes spilled all over the floor. "I went to an auction at the performing arts center in the city today because they were auctioning off old furniture and clothing they didn't think they would need any longer to raise money for new curtains. I went a little wild because prices were low and there weren't many bidders. I'm trying to get this Wyatt Earp type suit on this mannequin, and even with pulling the belt tight it keeps slipping down."

Nick asked the obvious question, "Where are the missing pieces? That is why the pants are falling down."

Fannie looked at him like he was crazy. "That's why this one was on sale for $2.00. I was going to figure out a way to fix it sometime and never got around to it."

"What a bargain," retorted Nick. Fannie and Nick held the pants and mannequin upright while Jean fashioned suspenders from yarn that was in the store.

"Come help me unload the rest of the van," ordered Fannie. The two walked obediently out the back door to see about a dozen boxes and a few pieces of furniture.

"What is in all the boxes?" asked Jean.

"More costumes, a real bargain at $5.00 per box for the things that didn't sell individually," Fannie said with a lot of joy. "The hat and guns should be in one of those boxes. I might not even put them out. You know how I hate guns." Fannie said.

Jean, seeing Nick tilting his head towards the door, ended the stay with a promise, "I will come help unpack the boxes Monday." With a look around, Jean decided to extend the offer, "I'll help some each day until we get it done."

Right then, Jean's phone rang. Seeing Priscilla's number, she answered immediately. "Is everything ok?" After a few one word comments like ok and right, Jean hung up the phone.

"Why wouldn't everything be ok?" asked Fannie.

"Priscilla left early today a little upset. She said her son-in-law came home last night, packed his clothes and left. Her daughter is very distraught over the surprise of his walking out and called her for help today. She will give a full report on Monday at water aerobics, which sounds like it will be water therapy instead. I will tell you when I know more," Jean said as she walked out the door.

Jean turned to Nick and gave him a little quick kiss, "You've been wonderful today."

Nick smiled, "Protect and Serve is the police motto. I defend against the killing of frogs and serve even the deformed mannequin kind."

Fannie stepped out as they kissed. "Gross!" she shouted. "If you're going to do something like that, I'm out of here." Fannie walked quickly away.

Jean turned back to Nick, "You deserve a treat. Why don't I throw a couple of things in the overnight bag? I need 15 minutes tops. We can head up the coast to our favorite restaurant and stay at the hotel that overlooks the water."

"Sounds like a great plan," said Nick as they started to the apartment.

As they turned the corner, which was in front of Belinda's house, her door came open. "Hi, so glad you are walking by. My husband fell on the stairs, and I need help getting him to the car. He wants to go to the hospital and get it checked out."

"Is he ok?" Jean asked with concern. Jean could hear a moan coming out of Nick.

Belinda smiled, "He's fine, a slight sprain of the ankle at the worst. Men can be such babies, so best to get it checked."

Nick placed a hand on Jean's back and whispered, "Here's the deal, I will help get him in the car if you go pack your bag."

Jean would not be deterred from helping a friend, "Do you need us to go with you to the hospital?"

"No, I'm sure you have better things to do," assured Belinda.

Nick pushed Jean lightly then headed up the steps, "Go! Run!" he said in a low voice as he headed up the steps to help the injured.

By the time Jean had the bag packed, Nick walked in the door. He grabbed the bag and took Jean's hand. "Quick before anyone interferes with the plan."

Jean laughed, ran out beside Nick and looked forward to the rest of the weekend.

Chapter 5 – Priscilla's Report

On Monday morning, Jean arrived back in town when she got a call from Fannie. "I'm joining you for water aerobics today." Jean gave a shocked look at the phone. Even though Fannie's store was closed on Monday, she never joined the group for most activities, especially time in the swimming pool.

"Okay," said Jean slowly.

Fannie inquired, "Is Priscilla going to be there? Will we hear what has happened?"

Jean now understood that Fannie wanted the story firsthand but still was unsure about Fannie's change of heart about letting someone see her in a swimming suit. "Yes, things are running on our normal schedule today, so we will be going to the pool about 2:00. You're welcome to join us for what I think will be water therapy."

The pool was located in the backyard at the Friend's Home. The proceeds from Jean's book, "Veiled Murder," paid the cost of the installation. Jean wrote the book years before but recently retold the story on the porch to her friends. Besides the fact that Jean loved to swim, many people at the home had doctors who suggested using a pool for improvement in joint movement caused by surgeries or arthritis. It was important for their health. Jean kept a key to the fence around the pool area and there was a second key behind the reception desk. Everyone including employees was invited to enjoy the pleasure of the pool. The pool could be reserved for special functions by filling in a calendar on a white board next to the key. Jean's water class was always at 2:00 Monday through Friday. Should the classes be cancelled for some reason, it would be written on the board.

Priscilla, Eve, Belinda, Jo and a few other residents were in the pool with Jean. She started calling out the movements. Running in place was always the start. When it was just about time to switch to wide leg jogging, everyone stopped and stared. Jean turned around then laughed long and loud. Fannie must have found a swimming suit circa 1915 in the costume box. The suit was dark gray in color with a top that looked like a dress, sleeves to the elbow, a round neck line, then gathered at the waist with a ribbon. The bottom portion was pantaloons with strips of the ribbon going around the legs three times. Topping off the outfit was a hat gathered in a full style in which Fannie's blonde hair was tucked up safe from the chlorine. The same ribbon wove through the hat so it could be pulled tight. Even Fannie's feet were fully covered with bathing shoes.

"Have I missed anything yet? Priscilla, are you okay?" Fannie's voice showed true concern for her friend as she jumped into the pool.

Trying to restore order to the class, Jean suggested, "Let's go to wide leg jog and let Priscilla start her story. I admit to being very curious too."

Priscilla hadn't said a word to anyone and looked like she could cry. "My son-in-law left my daughter. He showed up about midnight on Friday night, after the boys were in bed, announced he is in love with someone else, walked into the bedroom and packed a couple of suitcases. Richard then said he would send for the rest of his things later and just walked out. Kathy tried to keep her crying as silent as possible to not wake up their two sons. Kathy ran to the computer to lock their bank accounts and found Richard already moved half the money. Money that Richard didn't earn, he just stole it! Kathy called me early Saturday asking me to come up. She didn't know what to say to the boys. She didn't sleep all night and was exhausted. We let the boys sleep as long as possible then served breakfast. Jerry asked where his father was but we said we didn't know for sure. When breakfast was over, we sat down and told them what little we knew; not about taking the money but him showing up, making his announcement, and then walking out. We tried to be honest but not say anything bad. Jerry, bellowing at his mother, asked what we did to make his father leave. We told him we didn't do anything. Jerry ran to his room crying and wouldn't speak to us. Craig just went over and started playing video games. Kathy asked him if he was ok. He just shrugged his shoulders and said he was tired of his dad being grumpy and at last they would have peace."

Priscilla started to cry some. "I guess it might be good to tell those of you that don't know Kathy a little about her. She started a business teaching people to swim, kayak, canoe, and paddle board close to the marina. Kathy always did competitive swimming and was getting paid for doing things she loved. Kathy has such a great personality that people liked and trusted her. She could get someone afraid of the water to swim like a fish in just a few lessons. Business was so good that she had to start hiring staff to help but Kathy was involved with all the customers. I'm sure Richard was attracted to her not just because of her good looks and personality but because she was making good money. Richard said he was a dance teacher but seldom had customers and brought in very little money.

About two years ago, a drunken boater lost control and was headed straight to where Kathy had some people on paddle boards. Kathy pushed one girl out of the way and then tried to jump to safety, but the boat hit her and injured her lower spine. She can now move with a walker, but there was a time while in rehab where she used a wheelchair. The boater got away with no one catching the number on the side of the boat. Insurance paid for her hospital stay, operations and even the cost of the wheelchair and lift for the car. The money wasn't enough for them to live on for long. Kathy was trying to get on disability but the paperwork takes time.

Kathy asked Richard to take over the business. His rudeness ran off not only the customers but also the employees. Within a year, they were in bankruptcy and the equipment was sold to pay creditors. All he had to do was show up and not screw up because the staff was great. Even if he stayed away, the staff could have handled it but he was mad because Kathy asked him to actually work to earn an income and support his family.

The disability check arrived and was a very nice size because of it being backdated to the start of the application date. Now he took half! This was Kathy's money, not his! I never did like him but was nice to him for Kathy's sake. He was the biggest mistake of her life. He was never there for Kathy. He complained if she asked for help. Now Jerry acts like he is in shock, and I'm worried about all of them."

Priscilla left the pool crying.

Chapter 6 – Introducing Patty

No one knew what to do. Should they go after Priscilla? It was decided to give her time to cry alone. Then Jean, who was her best friend and next door neighbor, would go over to check on her. The class ended with everyone feeling sad in spite of hearing the frog story from Eve and Jo. Fannie told the story of the no hip mannequin. Belinda updated on her husband's hospital visit, along with her plan to be away from the house due to his constant asking to be babied because of the sprained ankle. "With the boot he gets along fine. Besides, it is more a slight twist rather than a full sprain," said Belinda.

Around 5:30, Jean took two plates of food to Priscilla's room. Priscilla never ate much, had zero body fat, and the chances of her eating were slim. After Jean ate her meal and Priscilla picked at her food, Jean suggested they sit outside in the chairs under the tree so they could talk without being overheard. The neighbor on the other side of Priscilla's apartment was known as Nosey Rosie. Many suspected Rosie would listen through doors and walls to get gossip on the other housemates but she could be nice and supportive of people with troubles. Rather than confront Rosie about the errors of her eavesdropping, the house residents just didn't talk where they could be overhead.

Jean and Priscilla picked up their plates to drop them off in the kitchen on their way out. Priscilla didn't want to go into the kitchen because Chef Dan would scold her for not eating. The truth was Chef Dan did have a secret mission to put a little weight on Priscilla. It was an insult to his cooking as well as a concern over Priscilla's health. He often planned his meals to give her the right healthy nutrients that she needed. As Priscilla handed over the plate, Chef Dan gave her a hug, "You must eat to stay healthy. Your daughter and grandsons need you. You must eat and stay strong for them."

"I'll try to eat more tomorrow," Priscilla promised.

Settled in chairs under a shade tree surrounded by a beautiful garden, Jean tried to think carefully about how to start. "On Friday night, Nick and I went dancing. We saw Richard with a woman on the dance floor. He didn't see us for some time so I had a long time to observe them. When Richard finally saw us, he grabbed the girl's arm and started to leave. One last glance over his shoulder, he saw me starring at them with a hard look on my face. Richard then waved and approached with the girl on his arm. Introductions were made like we were old friends. Patty was introduced as one of Richard's dance students that he was taking out for a real life experience, not the controlled class dancing environment, because she was going to be dancing at a relative's wedding. Nick invited them to join us and I made a point of sitting so Patty and I could talk. Richard tried to keep the conversation limited by saying he and Patty needed to be on the dance floor. He would let the tired girl rest when Nick and I got up. It became a game of keep away."

Priscilla didn't speak and just stared at Jean's face as she spoke. Priscilla wanted the bottom line of Jean's thoughts and sometimes the best way was to let her tell the full story.

Jean continued, "I knew right away that we caught Richard cheating on his wife. Nick said we didn't have any evidence. Patty told me Richard was going to the wedding with her. When I pointed out, nicely of course, that Richard was married, she told me the usual cheating man lines that he had told her. Things like, 'His wife didn't understand him,' 'They haven't had a relationship in years,' and the classic, 'I never cheated on my wife before but I've fallen so in love with you.' Of course, on that one he added, 'I'm so confused. I want to do the right thing but can't help how my heart feels.' This girl is in her late 20's but never had a boyfriend. She is so desperate for attention that she is willing to believe anything. Maturity-wise, I would say she is more like 17 with no real life experiences to open her eyes to the truth."

"Do you think they are having an affair?" asked Priscilla. "Who is she? What does she look like?"

Nick warned Jean about jumping to conclusions or saying things she didn't know as facts, but Jean had to be honest with Priscilla. They were best friends. "I don't know their status, but my hunch is that he was playing her for some reason. Now that he deserted his wife and kids, I would say my hunch is confirmed. When she told me her full name, I realized that she is an heir to a fortune. She is the only granddaughter of a very wealthy man that lives near Belinda's parents. The great-grandfather made a ton of money as an industrialist in the 1800's. The old man taught his son, Alex, good investment strategy. Alex had one daughter, who is Patty's mom. Alex and Barb, his wife, were caring for the granddaughter, Patty, so Patty's parent could celebrate their 10th anniversary. Patty's parents died that day in a car wreck. Patty was all the family the grandparents had left. Alex and Barb did the best they could to raise their granddaughter but were overly protective. Patty couldn't leave the house without one of them with her. She was in a private school with only 5 to 10 other rich kids in the class. Patty never got over the loneliness she felt at the loss of her parents, and I think she is craving someone to love her; someone older to replace the loss of the father she worshiped. I think Richard is only about 10 years older but that would be enough. As for her looks, she is very homely. Patty has no taste in clothes. Buying expensive doesn't relate to good taste. Basically, I think Richard is going after her because he is a gold digger. He has no intentions of working or being a responsible man. Richard is a spoiled, self-serving leech. Sorry, I got carried away there." Jean quickly apologized. "I can hear Nick's voice getting on me and he's not even here. That is scary, his common sense intruding in my emotional outbursts."

Priscilla had to laugh out loud on that one. Jean was determined to remain single after her disaster of a marriage years before. The single status worked for over 30 years when she and Nick ran into each other during a mystery. Now they have a permanent relationship with respectable boundaries.

Priscilla, still a little more relaxed, said, "I think you have it right on all accounts. Kathy suspected Richard of cheating on her the whole time they were married. She didn't have proof but really didn't dig too hard to find any. As long as he was good to the boys and faked being nice to her, she was ok living life that way. They didn't have a relationship as friends and confidents, but what they had was good enough as long as Kathy had a successful business and didn't bother him too much. Richard was much closer to the older son, Jerry, but my youngest grandson doesn't really like being around his dad. I guess there is nothing to do but get a good lawyer and get things down in writing on how to live life from this day forward in the form of a property settlement agreement and divorce."

"Are you going back to Kathy's house?" asked Jean. Priscilla shook her head no.

"Kathy appreciates me being there but feels she and the boys have to create a new normal routine. She promised to call if she needs me. I told her to call anytime, day or night, and I would be there instantly. I even offered to sleep with my street clothes on instead of a gown, but she just laughed and assured me there wouldn't be anything that couldn't wait the extra 5 minutes for me to get dressed."

Jean told the stories that Priscilla missed of the frog plague, the no hip mannequin, and the falling husband. Jean was good with stories and maximized the humor to keep Priscilla laughing. Jean invited Priscilla to join her in the morning to help Fannie go through the boxes she bought at the auction. The normal routine of the house was for Jean to get up at 9, eat breakfast and go to the porch for stories. "Tomorrow, I plan to make a huge sacrifice and will get up at 8 and be at Fannie's store by 9. Jo is taking over story time and will join us for tea." Priscilla was an early riser and was fine with the time and grateful for the distraction.

Chapter 7 – Fannie's Wardrobe

Fannie proudly considered herself an American Bohemian. Other people used various terms for her like unconventional, artistic, and even eccentric. Fannie Annie actually went out of her way to do things so people would talk. She considered being on people's tongues as a form of good advertising. When people finally accepted Fannie's odd behavior, it was like giving her a license to act even stranger.

Jean and Priscilla entered to see Fannie had been hard at work for a long while. "Where have you been? I thought you said you would come early to help today."

Jean, looking at Fannie who was dressed as Cleopatra, shook her head in disbelief, before she replied, "This is early for me and as early as I can take your surprises of the day."

Fannie turned shocked, "What do you mean surprises? Are you expecting something unusual?"

Jean walked to the area of the store in which she stored her tea and began making a cup. Talking in a monotone voice, Jean began, "I guess if you don't think someone dressed in a long golden gown with her head covered in a wig of gold that has a bird carving in it, with a fake asp on her shoulder and a glittery wrap around her arms as unusual or surprising, then let's just say this is a normal day so far. I just have a feeling things could go in an odd direction from here."

Fannie, very pleased at her friend's wit and refusal to have a reaction to her dress, decided to kick it up a little. "Jean, you need something to go with the tea. I'm going to pop into the bakery next door to see what smells so good and get you some of it." Fannie exited her store and walking down the street with one arm extend to the front, palm up at neck level and the other arm to the back with the hand pointed at hip level, moved the arms in and out with each step of the shuffle to the building next door.

Fannie's entrance was welcomed with stares. Buddy had just taken a bite and began choking on the food. His wife, Gloria, stopped serving customers long enough to pound on Buddy's back and asked, "What can we do for you today?"

The room remained totally silent as Fannie smiled at Gloria. "Jean and Priscilla are next door planning to help me, but Jean is a little crabby so I thought something sweet might help."

Gloria reached for a box and put a cheese Danish in it for Jean and two cherry pastries for Fannie and Priscilla. "I think this might do the trick."

As Gloria collected the money, she finally gave in to Fannie's desire to talk about the outfit. "Nice outfit, Fannie. Do you think it might be a little out of style?"

Fannie, delighted with the opening, replied, "I think it is just right for me. What do you think, Buddy? Would you like to see my asp?"

Buddy naturally thought she said ass and turned beet red. Before Buddy could reply, Fannie flung her shoulder cover to the side to reveal the fake snake. Gloria laughed, and Buddy walked away, not speaking, to the back room. The previously quiet crowd erupted with laughter. Fannie exited with her right arm in position with the palm up in front of her with the box balanced on it and the other arm behind her with the palm down.

Jean and Priscilla, who had gone outside to witness the whole show, ran back into the store acting nonchalant as Fannie came in with a wide smile on her face. "Well done. Got the town talking now and got back on Buddy's naughty list. I guess you are so proud," Jean greeted.

Fannie couldn't hold back the laughter any longer and the others had to join in. "You have to wait and see what I have planned this week, but no previews. Let's eat and get started."

Fannie was telling Priscilla and Jean about what she discovered in the first few boxes. "The clothing content is a little outlandish for everyday use, so I think I am going to set up a rental section in the back of the store. I will rent them as is with no alternation." Jean thought that was a good idea because Fannie didn't sew and she knew who would get stuck doing the work.

For the remainder of the morning, the three worked hard clearing out a spot in the back corner. They then set up racks for the clothing. The end of work was putting together a wrought iron fence around the section to separate the rentals from the rest of the store. Exhausted from all the hot hard labor, Priscilla and Jean headed back to their apartments for lunch, rest and to get ready for water aerobics.

The talk of the water class was the Fannie show of the day and the changes at her store. Many of the ladies had heard the story secondhand as it quickly spread around the usually quiet town. Belinda and Eve felt left out so they volunteered to join Priscilla and Jean at 8:30 the next morning at Fannie's to help with the remaining work.

Chapter 8 – Costumes Continued

Priscilla, Jean and Belinda entered Fannie's store, the Attic. They were not disappointed because they could tell it would be an eventful day. Fannie was dressed in a full skirt that showed white lace when she moved, white stocking, black shoes, and a white peasant blouse with a brocade vest. Fannie's hair was in a short bob and she was singing loudly.

Jean turned and used her sarcastic tone of voice, "Oh, we are in luck! Did you know Fannie knows the entire score of 'The Sound of Music?'"

Fannie, in an effort to be annoying, sang even louder.

Jean continued, "Fannie, you don't want us to work on an empty stomach, do you? Why don't you go see Buddy and Gloria? They usually sell scones on Wednesday."

Fannie smiled, obviously loving the idea, "I'll be right back."

The trip next door was not only Fannie singing loudly but dancing with odd steps she thought would go good with the song. The dance looked more like a Scottish jig but Fannie didn't care. She entered the bakery and danced around the room before going to the counter. By that time, Buddy had escaped to the kitchen and Gloria was laughing. "You are really good for business. Customers are coming just to see what you will be wearing next."

Fannie, cheerful as always, replied, "So glad I could help." The order was placed and paid for before the big exit. Singing 'You Never Walk Alone' as she stepped onto the sidewalk just missing Eve's feet, Fannie threw her arm around the friend. Eve at first was taken back but recovered in time to join the singing.

Eve was carrying a large cloth bag filled with papers which she threw onto the floor next to the restroom door. "What's in the bag?" asked Belinda.

"Paperwork for the law office two blocks down. I thought I would head there after we worked a while and didn't want to have to walk back home to get it." Breakfast was consumed so it was time for the work to begin.

Fannie already had one load of wash completed in her upstairs apartment so Priscilla and Jean started ironing. Belinda and Eve were working on the washing, drying, and hanging the clothes on the racks by sizes. The store was very busy that morning so Fannie worked on signs to go on the wrought iron between waiting on customers. Jean's phone rang so she exited the store to take the call. Belinda took over the ironing duties.

Jo entered the store and said she had news to tell after she used the restroom. Seconds later, a loud scream was heard throughout the store that came from the restroom. Jo exited quickly, pulling up her pants as she hurried out. "Something is in there and it just fell on my head. It was like a plop on the top of my head and this rubbery floppy thing on my forehead and nose." Jo looked back in the restroom and saw a tree frog sitting on the center of the floor. "Did you fall on my head?" Jo continued talking to the frog, "Are you ok? You scared me. I bet you are scared too."

The others came over and peered inside. "Go! Get it out!" yelled Eve.

"Not me. Where is Jean?" replied Jo.

Fannie said that Jean left the store a few minutes ago on a phone call.

"I'm not afraid," said Belinda. "Just let me go into the laundry room and get a few things."

Jean walked in to a call of "WHERE HAVE YOU BEEN?" by the group collectively. Right then, Belinda descended down the stairs armed for battle. Goggles covered Belinda's eyes, an apron over her clothes, yellow rubber gloves that came to her elbows to protect her hands and arms, and in her hands were a toilet bowl brush and a bucket.

Too stunned for words, Jean's mouth hung open with her eyes in a wide stare. All of a sudden, the laughter came and Jean laughed until she had tears in her eyes. "Are you trying to outdo Fannie on strange outfit of the day? 'The Man from La Mancha' for the housewife set? Are you going to war armed with a toilet bowl brush?"

Jean didn't understand why she was the only one laughing. Belinda's hands went to her hips as she sternly addressed Jean, "While you were out gallivanting around, we had a crisis. A frog plopped on Jo's head when she was going to the bathroom and it's still in there. I was going to be brave enough to remove it."

Jean looked at her sister, Jo, who confirmed the story, "Right here on top of my head and it's leg went down my face."

Not even trying to suppress the enjoyment of the events, Jean asked, "So when you didn't scare the frog to death with your scream, you decided to have the cleaner from the Black Lagoon enter to finish the job off. You all realize this is going in a book one day." Jean actually did incorporate some of the adventures into her writing so the threat was not an idle one.

Eve could hold back no longer, "There's a frog in there! We need to call the humane society!"

Jean walked over, opened the door and picked up the frog. Looking nose-to-nose with the creature, she said, "You look more mad then scared. Are these women picking on you? I will take you someplace safe. There's a nice pool at Eve's house you can swim in."

Jo piped up, "That was the good news I had to tell you. I got Michael to take the pool apart and to make sure all the frogs were removed."

Jean said, "No worries, there are a lot more places we can go." She left the store shouting over her shoulder, "Get back to work, ladies. This is too much excitement coming here every day." Jean brought the phone to her face and began snapping pictures of the friends, the frog and Belinda's lovely outfit.

The boxes were about 70% empty so the friends all departed to get ready for pool time. "I have to be in the pool to defend myself. Hard to say what stories Jean will tell the others," said Belinda. Fannie gave everyone a hug goodbye, said the proper thank you and promised tomorrow would be their last day if everyone would please return.

Chapter 9 – .45 Colt

Priscilla, Belinda, Jo and Jean all arrived at the same time. Eve begged off saying she had too much work and had to pay attention to her accounting business. Fannie was in jeans, a black t-shirt, boots and a black leather jacket. Her song and dance let the other's know they just walked into the set of 'West Side Story'. She was moving, snapping her fingers, then singing the song 'Maria'. The others decided to join her on the trip next door doing the same stooped over moves and snapping their fingers. The bakery erupted in laughter and many got out of their seats to join the parade around the eating area. Gloria was enjoying the show but blocked Buddy from his retreat to the kitchen. "Remember when we thought that movie was cool?" Gloria asked Buddy.

Breakfast was ordered, paid for, and then the gang began to exit. Jean shouts as she exits, "Tomorrow,

Fannie assures me the costume will be based on the play 'Hair.'"

This was one of the few times the town saw Fannie flustered as she denied that 'lack of costume' would never be on the streets of the town. Fannie pulled Jean back over to the store.

"Glad to hear that won't happen," said Buddy.

Back at Fannie's store, they ate their breakfast, talked about the frog, and then it was back to work. There were very few boxes left and most were props to go with the costumes already in place. "It really looks good in here and so many great choices of things to wear," Belinda said.

Fannie, who was really a serious business woman, looked a little discouraged, "Yes, but it is a long time until Halloween and I would really like to recoup some of my expenses before that."

Belinda responded, "Oh, I know, my husband and I have these murder mystery games in which you have a dinner, everyone comes in costume, they draw the character cards, then everyone acts while they eat and have drinks afterward until the murderer is discovered. They are so much fun. I will start having a party about once a month. The parties should bring in some business because on the invitation I will make the suggestion to come here."

"Thanks so much. That is a great idea and sounds like fun. I hope I get invited to one of the parties," said Fannie.

"Last thing in the last box," said Priscilla.

Fannie went over to lift it out. "These are the guns and holster for the Wyatt Earp outfit in the store window." A curious look came over Fannie's face as she lifted the holster. "This is very heavy on one side and very light on the other."

Priscilla inspected the guns, "One is a toy .45 Colt but the other appears to be real."

As Priscilla slipped the gun from the holster, it was Jo that became nervous, "Maybe we shouldn't handle that. Maybe we should call Nick to look at it."

Priscilla assured Jo that her ex-husband always owned guns and while Priscilla didn't know much about them, she knew how to be careful. Priscilla gripped the top of the gun with the handle in the air and the barrel pointed to the floor, flipped open the cover and turned the cylinder. "This looks real and it appears to be loaded. What are we going to do with it?"

Fannie hated guns as much as Jo so she didn't want to have it anywhere near. "Besides," Fannie said, "I don't think I'm permitted to sell guns."

Jean was already at the computer pulling up the website and called to Priscilla, "What is the serial number?"

Priscilla read it off. "You know, this gun looks like it's in really good condition."

Jean inquired, "Is that an ivory handle with engraving?"

"Yes, it looks like it. I don't know if it is real or fake," said Fannie.

Jean looked up surprised, "You better hope it is real, Fannie. The serial number appears to be from 1878 and only about 1% of the guns were engraved back then. This gun, if real, is worth a lot of money." That got Fannie's attention and she joined Jean as they searched the internet for more information on value and signs for authenticity.

Jean suggested, "Why don't you lock it in the drawer behind the desk? Guests never go back there. It will be locked up and no one will know that it is there except us."

Fannie, though realizing it might be a great financial benefit, was still worried. "Real antique guns aren't used as stage props. I'm worried about the implications that this might be stolen and I'm involved."

Jean continued, "Nick will be down tomorrow. It doesn't hurt to keep it locked up and ask him about it when he comes. He might know if it is real and he can check to see if it is on the stolen list anywhere. I guess they have a stolen gun list. There's nothing else we can do. You bought it fairly at the auction so you might end up making your money back and more."

Fannie agreed. The gun was wrapped up in a cloth bag, placed in the drawer, shut very carefully and then locked. The key to the drawer was then hidden on a hook in the back room. Glad that the project was complete, the other ladies headed for the pool. Fannie was standing guard over the gun when customers arrived and she finally started to relax. No one knew it was there. It would be fine.

Chapter 10 – Body Discovered

Nick and his partner, Detective Janice Hoover, were looking at the clock wishing time would move faster. They worked hard all week and the case load was to the point that they could go home and enjoy the weekend. The head of the detectives opened his door and shouted their names.

"Really?" groaned Janice, "One hour left in the day. A call this late means a late night and possibly the weekend canceled."

Nick smiled, "I'm sure the victim didn't die just to ruin our weekend, even if that is the end result." Nick called Jean as he left to let her know that plans were canceled for tonight. "I'll call you tomorrow and let you know about the rest of the weekend."

They were handed the directions to the crime scene which was on the beach about an hour drive with rush hour traffic. They only knew that the body had washed ashore and there was no chance the victim could be saved.

As they approached the beach, there was a couple standing with a uniformed officer. "Hi," said the officer, "This is Mr. and Mrs. King. They were walking on the beach and noticed something odd floating in the water. Mr. King waded out and discovered the body floating face down. When he flipped her over, he saw a very gruesome sight."

Mrs. King, looking as if she had been crying, jumped into the conversation, "We just got married in Iowa and are here on our honeymoon. I can't believe something as negative as finding a body would happen. I'm so sorry for the woman but nothing will ever take away this horrible scene as the memory of the trip."

Mr. King hugged his wife closely. "We are staying at this hotel in room 338. We gave our statements to the officer. Can we at least go up to the bar and get something to drink to help calm our nerves?"

Nick said, "Thank you for calling the police. I'm so sorry for this incident. We will try not to keep you waiting too long. If you could, stay close until we have a chance to look things over just in case we have any other questions, I would appreciate it. A drink at the bar would be fine but I would appreciate you limiting yourselves to one while we look over the crime scene."

Janice and Nick could see three sets of tracks. One was where the couple had been walking closely together. They were so close, it indicated that the Kings were probably hugging as they walked. One set walking back out matched the foot prints that went in. There was also one set of footprints in shoes that went to the body that matched the shoes of the police officer. You could tell he walked in alone and tried to walk back out in his same steps. The officer explained the steps, which was not necessary but a part of his report, so the detectives listened quietly.

Nick and Janice walked in on the tracks of the officer and looked down at the body. Nick proposed that he say the facts out loud while Detective Hoover wrote them in the notebook. "Female, Caucasian, no face or finger prints left, dressed in name brand jeans and tee shirt that could be bought at any department store. Besides the missing face which the predators of the sea had removed, there appears to be a hole in the eye socket suggesting a bullet might still be lodged in the body. We need to follow up with the medical examiner on that. The body is of course a blue color and bloated, all suggesting a long time in the water. There is also a rope attached to the right ankle that is frayed at the end, suggesting the body had been tied down to a cinderblock brick and the motions of the waves moving the body finally got it to break. I don't see anything in the front pockets but we will let the coroner do the search for anything deep in the jeans. Do you see anything further we need to add for now?"

Even though both detectives had been in the business a long time and had seen the effects of the water on bodies before, that didn't make it any less nauseating to look at. Janice looked up, "Looks like the tech team has arrived. I don't see anything else to help our investigation. Why don't we just let them get about their job and hope they find something to help?"

The Kings were both pale and shaking when Nick and Janice walked up to them. "Let's just confirm the facts if you don't mind. Your statement says you were on a walk on the beach. You saw something floating in the water that looked like a piece of clothing. You, Mr. King, walked into the water, saw it was a woman and dragged her to shore. It appears no one else was on the beach at the time. Is that correct?"

"Yes," Mr. King answered. "We walked back to where we were standing with the officer. I had my wife sit down because I was afraid she might faint. I came here to the bar and asked the bartender to call. I went back to sit with my wife. We made sure no one else went that way because we knew that the police wouldn't want the area messed up and also because no one should have to see that horrific sight."

Nick, still in the lead of the conversation said, "You did everything just right. I want to say thank you. If you want to go to your room now and rest, it is very understandable."

The bartender walked by, "I'm the one that made the call but never went to the beach myself. I'm making sure they get all the free drinks they want."

Mrs. King looked worried, "There isn't a murderer at the hotel, is there? Do we have anything to worry about?"

Janice tried to look reassuring, "No ma'am, you will be fine. That body was in the ocean for at least a month and probably was out to sea, which is why it came in with the tide. You have nothing to be afraid of."

Mr. King asked, "Can we leave if we feel the need? We gave the officer our home address and phone number."

"Of course you can," assured Nick. "Look, we know you didn't have anything to do with the body, and we are sorry your trip hasn't been more pleasant."

Handshakes were exchanged as the couple left for their room and the detectives headed back to the office.

Chapter 11 – Richard's Mental Abuse

"Two weeks! I can't believe Nick hasn't been down here to see about the gun," Fannie complained to her friend Jean.

"Two weeks ago, he got involved in a case at the last minute and had to cancel, and last weekend we got great tickets for a game and we needed time away. I think he is afraid of all the action in this normally quiet town. I'm going up to his house tonight for dinner if he can get finished at the office early enough. I told him about the gun. He said the same thing I did about it: it was a proper purchase, it's old enough for you to have it in the store without a permit and he will inspect it later. No one else knows it's here and it hasn't caused any problems so why worry about it? Since Nick is working tomorrow, do you want me to go to the auction house with you?"

That made Fannie very happy. Fannie and Jean spent a lot of years traveling together and having fun. Jean, having a relationship with Nick, cut down on the hours she spent hanging out with Fannie. Jean liked being retired and spent a lot of time in solitude to do her writing. Fannie liked working and her hours were all spent at the store. Jean didn't mind stopping in each weekday but that was as much as she wanted to do. More customers just came in, so Jean used the excuse to head home.

Priscilla was sitting out under the trees, enjoying a glass of homemade lemonade. Jean sat down to catch up on the news. Since her son-in-law deserted the family, Priscilla spent a lot of days helping with the grandsons and house cleaning. There was an acknowledgement of Jean's arrival, but Priscilla looked very unhappy. "Do you want to talk? So what's wrong?" Jean opened the conversation being very straightforward as always.

Priscilla began to cry as she poured out the story. "I normally would be so glad the jerk was gone. I never did like him but my oldest grandson is taking it so hard. I'm worried about him." Jean listened but would make no comments so Priscilla could talk as she pleased. "The girlfriend that he calls 'Princess Patty' doesn't like kids. She doesn't do anything bad to them but basically ignores them. Richard tries to show what a man he is by yelling at and belittling the boys in front of her. He told my grandsons that this was their new mommy.

Jerry just hangs his head and doesn't speak but my youngest grandson Craig speaks up and told his dad, 'There is nothing wrong with the Mommy I have.' The other day, we were at one of Jerry's little league games and he wanted a hot dog. I said I would buy him one after he played, which I did. His dad came over and snatched it from his hands before he would take a bite and yelled, 'How can you ever make the pros eating this type of junk?' Jerry doesn't want to be a pro athlete. He just plays little league because his dad insists. While the game was going on, Princess P was running up and down the sidelines, cheering like she cared, with tight white slacks on that showed the black G-string she had on instead of underwear. This was not only embarrassing to see, but I heard other parents trying to explain to their kids why the woman's butt looked so funny."

Jerry also won a place on the debate team but didn't want to participate. The teacher talked to him to find out why and then called us in for a talk. The teacher began her talk hesitatingly, 'It appears that Jerry now thinks he is stupid. I, of course, told him he wasn't. I went over all his academic achievements as well as his popularity with his fellow students. He finally said he would participate but only if I made sure that none of his family would be present.' In just a couple of months, this boy went from being positive with unlimited potential to being a very big concern. The horrible man is destroying my grandson."

Jean reached over to pat Priscilla's shoulders. "I would like to say everything will be ok with your love as well as your daughter's and his brother's, but I'm concerned too. I really think you should go back to the teacher and seek her suggestions or that of the school counselor. I'm speaking from a voice of experience. I won't bore you with my story but I just want to say you need to be proactive in helping this kid get his self-esteem back. Make sure to document all that happens so if necessary it can be presented in court should things be so bad you need visitations controlled. What about Craig? Is he doing ok?"

Priscilla gave a slight smile. "He is a character. Being much younger, he has a different prospective of his father. My daughter and her husband have been fighting since shortly after he was born. She was trying to get the man to work and support his family. She was trying to get some help medically for the boys. That's all he remembers. My daughter worked and supported the family for years. Richard actually liked being with his son so he did a lot of the care with Jerry. He never had much interaction with Craig so there is no bond. The scary thing is, Richard is so busy with Princess P that he doesn't watch the kids or spend time with them even when they are at his house. Craig decided he wanted to go home one night and just left the house. The police found him a few blocks away at 3:00 in the morning. I'm just glad he decided to go home instead of going for a swim. When the police returned Craig to

Richard's house, he didn't even know his 4-year-old son was gone."

"At least that is on the police record," said Jean.

Priscilla was on a roll of venting so Jean kept the comment short and let her continue. "They took the boys to meet her grandparents that raised her as a daughter. Princess P told the boys that children were to be seen and not heard, so they better just sit quiet the whole time they were visiting. The boys are afraid not to comply. To their surprise, the grandfather was kind to them. He took them to the store and got them games to play and comic books to read. The grandmother had the cook bake cookies with them. They had a good time as long as Richard and Patty stayed out of the room."

Priscilla looked at Jean worried, "My daughter has no money for a divorce attorney. Richard appears to have unlimited resources. Do you have any suggestions on what to do?"

Jean looked up the number for a team of female attorneys that specialized in helping women that had such battles and no resources. She also showed Priscilla the best way to document the problems and occurrences that had happened. Jean offered, "If you need someone to spend time with the boys, to help in any way possible, I will be glad to do so. I think it is best for the boys not to be around when the divorce debates occur."

"I do have a very major favor to ask of you and my other friends," Priscilla said grimly. "Jerry's birthday is next Saturday. He will be 12. He wants a pool party."

Jean smiled, "Great. We can have a really nice party for him here."

Priscilla continued, "The problem is he wants his father to be there."

Jean's eyes widened, "You did explain that even though they are still legally married, they are no longer a family and he gets two parties instead of one, right?"

Priscilla shook her head no. "I tried to tell Kathy that, but she is too worried about Jerry being upset that she feels it would be best to include him. She and I can tolerate a couple of hours with the princess and the frog rather than telling Jerry they can't come. His dad appears to be all for it so Kathy would look like the bad person if she refused."

"Ok," Jean said not looking happy, "I don't agree with the arrangements but I said I would be supportive. Jerry might be holding out hope that his parents will get back together but it is wrong to let that hope live. I will make sure the whole gang is here, especially Nick."

Priscilla reacted, "Why? There won't be any trouble, I promise."

Jean smiled again, "You can only promise for yourself. You never know when I will go ballistic and say what's on my mind. Nick is pretty good about seeing when the explosion is coming and getting me to control my temper."

This was Priscilla's turn to laugh, "You? I've known you for years and never saw you lose you temper, not even once." No comment from Jean on that point.

Priscilla reached over and touched Jean's arm, "Thanks, Jean. I truly appreciate your support. I try to stay positive. I look for anything funny to tell them. At least Fannie gave me lots of material for a while."

Chapter 12 – The Robbery

On Saturday morning, the much too loud ringing of the phone awoke Jean from a very sound sleep. "Are you in bed alone?"

Jean, trying to focus and look at the clock, asked, "Fannie, is that you?"

"Of course it is! Knowing how grumpy you are in the morning, who else would call you this early? Are you alone or is Nick with you?"

Jean, wide awake by this time, replied, "I don't think that's any of your business." Nick was starting to stir beside her.

"It has to be Fannie," he moaned. Jean shook her head yes.

"I need you down here right away," said Fannie almost in tears.

Jean starting to realize the panic in Fannie's voice and responded as a good friend should. "What's wrong,

Fannie?" After listening a minute, Jean said, "Don't go in there. We will be there right away."

Jean was already up and dressed in two minutes so Nick knew it was a real emergency. "What's going on?" he asked as he put on his clothes, finishing at the same time as Jean.

"Fannie said the back door to the Attic was unlocked. She knows she locked it last night when she left. There are scratch marks around the lock so she is sure someone broke it."

After hearing that, Nick grabbed his gun as they started out the door. "So much for thinking this is a sleepy little town. Every time I come down, there seems to be a crisis. I really don't think that you coming along with me is the best plan."

Jean shot him a determined look but said nothing, as she matched his stride as they ran down the street.

Fannie did follow instructions and remained outside the door a few steps away. "Maybe I should have called the local police to back you up. I didn't know what to do. If I called the police and there was no reason to do so, they might think I'm crazy."

"Too late for that," said Jean.

"For what?" replied Fannie, "To call in backup?"

"No," replied Jean, "All the local people know you're crazy." To Nick, Jean asked, "What do you think? Do you need backup?"

Nick drew his gun. "I've got you, dear. We will be fine. Wait here with Fannie while I go in and look around." Nick returned in just minutes but for Jean it seemed like a really long time. "All clear," he reported. "Fannie and Jean, without touching anything, please come in, walk around the store, and see if anything is missing or disturbed."

Nick was looking in wonder as the two friends entered and did what they were told. It was a very unusual thing for either of them to listen to instructions, let alone both of them at the same time. He never saw them so serious. There was no joking or banter, just a very careful inspection of the room. "I don't see anything disturbed or missing," said Fannie.

Jean nodded in agreement but then changed her expression, "What about the gun?" Jean directed Nick to the drawer. "The key hangs in the backroom over the microwave." They walked to the room and the key was in its place. Nick reached for the key when Jean grabbed his arm. "What about fingerprints?"

Nick started to laugh. "You watch too many crime shows. Remember, they are not reality. You can't lift a usable print off every surface and we don't know if the gun is missing unless we open the drawer." Jean ran and got powder from the bathroom area and dusted the key as Nick laughed and shook his head. The key didn't have any prints because the surface has an old fashioned texture and prints wouldn't show. He took the key and used a cloth to open the drawer on the side in case there were prints on the handle. The holster was there but the gun was missing.

Nick then called the local police to let them know what was going on. The gun, if really old like Jean thought, would be valuable, plus you need to always report a stolen gun. The remainder of the morning was spent asking questions and the police inspecting the store. The handle of the drawer was wiped clean but that was the only thing disturbed in the store.

Fannie was able to reopen for business in a few hours. At the suggestion of the police, a locksmith arrived and removed the antique locks from the store and replaced them with the top- of-the-line deadbolts. Fannie hated the change because she tried to keep the building as close to its hundred-year-old look as possible but she realized how easy it was to pick the lock and wanted to feel more secure.

Chapter 13 – Pool Party

The party was to begin at 2:00 that afternoon. Over breakfast, Jean caught Nick up to speed on the pending divorce situation. She omitted the confession she made to Priscilla that she needed Nick to help keep her from saying anything that might escalate the existing problems but he inserted that thought on his own. "Am I in charge of making sure you don't get up and tell them off or do anything foolish?"

Jean smiled and agreed. "I just don't understand how that man could show his face at the party. He should be embarrassed and hiding in shame but instead he is strutting around like he is so wonderful. Maybe I should have told him off when he ruined the business, didn't support his wife and when we caught him cheating the night before he took off. I think sometimes a person needs reality thrown in their face so they can see how other people view them."

Nick took Jean's hand, "Believe me, if someone doesn't see the reality, they won't see it when you tell it to them. They are in their own world. That's why people that commit murder sometimes feel justified in doing so, especially in the moment. Maybe a year or so later sitting in a prison cell, they see things differently but most of the criminals still don't see it and feel justified in their actions."

Nick and Jean went to the pool area to help Priscilla with the preparations. Nick was in charge of setting up the seating and getting the grill prepared. Jean was helping Priscilla with the food when Belinda and her husband arrived with the cake. The guest list included more of Priscilla's friends than Jerry's. Kathy arrived with the boys about the same time that three couples arrived with their children. The children were Jerry's friends and all wanted to get into the pool immediately. Belinda and Steve offered to take first shift as life guards so the fun could start right away. Eve and Jo, with their spouses, arrived to add their support to Priscilla and Kathy. Eve and Nigel took control of the drink area, making up the tea and lemonade orders.

Then those considered the negative delegation, in Jean's opinion, arrived, which included not only Richard and Princess P, but the unexpected presence of his parents, Charles and Helen ReSol. Walking out toward the pool, the younger guests gravitated to the bar area on the right. The grill area was straight across the pool, now taken care of by Nick and Michael. The ReSol group went to the tables and chairs to the left to separate themselves from the other guests. Fannie arrived in her turn-of-the-century bathing suit and immediately sat next to Charles. Helen shot a dirty look at Fannie with the negative comment, "The height of fashion, are we? I hear what a spectacle you've been making of yourself around town."

Fannie just smiled and laughed. "Someone has to keep this town alive, so why not me?"

On the other side of Helen sat Richard, then Patty, who was quickly joined by Belinda. Josephine managed to get a chair in between Helen and Richard. Richard hated his stepmother so was quick to enter into a conversation with Josephine to avoid talking to Helen. Priscilla and Steve were now on lifeguard duty. Jean was going around checking on guests to see if they needed their drinks refreshed and offered appetizers.

Jean, extending the tray towards Charles and Helen asked, "Appetizers? I guess in your case I should say hors-d'oeuvr?"

Fannie immediately jumped on the opportunity to say, "France, I've been there many times. Parlez vous francais?"

Charles admitted, "I've never been to France. Our relatives came over many generations ago."

Fannie, with a confused look, said, "You don't speak French in the home? I thought with Richard pronouncing his name 'Ri-chard' that your French heritage was practiced at home."

Helen and Richard both shot her a dirty look. Charles, so glad to have a younger woman flirting with him, was even more drawn into the conversation. "I take it you don't come from old money then?" Fannie inquired.

Charles smiled and said, "I was born dirt poor. In my youth, I came up with the designs for making rubber belts for machinery and filed patents on those ideas. I didn't have success until my later years and now I'm very wealthy." Charles then proceeded to go over the development of his ideas, which Fannie appeared to be very interested in while Helen sat fuming.

Jo asked about dance lessons to occupy Richard but had to fake any interest since she hated to dance.

Belinda's parents were actually good friends with Patty's grandparents and the two were in a deep conversation about the local playhouse productions and mutual friends. Richard kept a nervous eye on Patty, afraid she would say something wrong.

Michael came over and handed Nick a drink in a dark colored plastic glass. His choice of container being plastic because of keeping the place around the pool safe and dark to hide the beer that was in the cup. Nick smiled, "This will help keep a hot chef cooler." He looked up and stared, "What is going on here?" Michael didn't understand so Nick explained, "It is normal for people to gravitate to their friends or people with similar interests. You have the group of parents on one side and what Jean is calling the evil ones on the right but Priscilla's friends are intermixed with the evil group."

Michael laughed, "You didn't get to hear about the planning session? It was at my house but I made myself scarce as soon as I could. I knew I would be designated a job anyway so I figured I didn't want to hear about the rest. The ladies did discuss the menu and decorations but they also made a plan to sit in what they considered would be the trouble spots. Each woman had her assignment on who they would try to control."

Nick just shook his head. This was not a surprise, and even if Michael made it sound like all the ladies were in on it, he had no doubt it was Jean in control.

After the meal and everyone resumed their assignments, Charles began to tell Fannie about all the patent ideas and his rise to success for the third time. Fannie acted like each time was the first time she heard it.

Richard had Michael with Josephine working on dance steps and lesson ideas.

Belinda was inquiring about the dancing at the relative's wedding that Patty and Richard claimed to be working on the night Jean first discovered their affair. Patty began the normal excuses like, "Kathy just doesn't understand Richard. He was so miserable, and after we were together, he had to make the break from his wife because he realized it was me he loved."

Helen joined in the conversation with Belinda, adding her viewpoint, "Kathy and her family are so much below our station in life. I was able to join Patty and Richard at her grandparent's and we have so much more in common with them." This conversation was overheard by Priscilla who flinched. Steve reached out and took her hand in comfort. Belinda noticed and appreciated that her husband had compassion for others.

The long afternoon in the sun was making everyone a little tired, but the day seemed to have taken its toll on Charles. He was still talking to Fannie when he said, "Per stirpes is bad."

Fannie looked confused, "What is per stirpes?"

"I don't know," Charles replied, "I just know per stirpes is bad."

Jean turned quickly when she heard him say this, spilling a couple of drinks on the tray. Helen turned to see the spill when Jean made direct eye contact with her and held the stare. Nick, seeing the event, hurried over to help with cleanup. "What's wrong with you?" he whispered.

"We will talk later," Jean whispered back.

Charles was repeating everything he just said, not even realizing the spill had occurred.

Helen jumped up and said, "We really must be leaving now."

Richard and Patty followed his parents out while trying to determine why Helen was so upset.

Helen explained, "Your dad isn't feeling up to his usual self and I just noticed how tired he was. I wouldn't be a good wife if I let him overdo it and get sick."

The other guests decided it was about time for the day to end also and made their way to the door. The friends began the cleanup. Jean and Fannie stepped aside. "Jean, you know that I worked as the entertainment director for a dementia ward at a nursing home. Charles has all the signs. He must still be functioning ok at home but it really showed as the day went on. I don't know what he was talking about when he said 'Per stirpes is bad.' Do you?"

"Yes, but I don't know why yet," Jean answered as she walked away.

All the friends were saying goodnight. Priscilla hugged each one thanking them for their help and for the support they gave her. Kathy and Priscilla were truly moved by the kindness of their friends. Even Jerry was giving hugs and grateful for the good day.

That night, as Nick and Jean were getting into bed, Jean told Nick of her gut feelings. "Helen is up to no good. I think she is about to do something wrong." The lights were out so they couldn't see each other's faces.

Nick was a little short with his comment, "You just don't like her and are imagining things. I think you are creating ideas like you do for your own crime novels," Jean's temper flared. She didn't answer but turned over and pretended to be asleep.

Chapter 14 – Nick Interviews Fannie

On the Monday after the party, the topic on the porch was a recap. The party went well, the grandson was happy, no one managed to start a fight, even though Jean felt it was due to the hosting team's interference. Helen's comments about the station in life was grating on Priscilla's mind. "The woman was poor and working in a bar when she married Charles. There is nothing wrong with that but she has no station in life. I actually pity Patty if she thinks Richard loves her. He is just using her for her money." The friends were all in agreement but there was nothing to be said or done to change the situation.

After talking in the morning, Jo, Jean, Priscilla and Belinda headed to the Attic. It was not open on Monday but the tea party was always held anyway. Jean was waiting until they were in the privacy of the store to approach a subject carefully in order to not create a false rumor. "Is Charles doing ok? He seemed confused at the end. I just wondered if he is having any health problems."

Priscilla stated that she had not heard of any but that she always had limited contact with Helen and Charles, even when her son-in-law was living with her daughter. Belinda and Jo didn't notice since they were helping with the other guests and Charles was under Fannie's watchful eye. Fannie nodded her head yes. "Due to my past experience of working with dementia patients, I think there are definitely signs of a memory illness. I would guess at the early stages but it might be further along than that. I never met him before so I can't really judge. A person with a memory disorder can have good and bad days. I did notice that as he was getting tired, he was getting more confused."

Belinda turned to Jean, "I'm working on remodeling my parents' basement. Could you go down to the island with me and help with the staging? My nephew got the new flooring put in and the walls painted. I brought a serving table and chairs from Fannie. She said you could drive them down in her van. I also plan to stop by the art show and pick up some paintings to bring everything together."

"When do you plan to go?" asked Jean.

"Since I'm asking the favor, I will let you pick but I hope to get it done in a couple of weeks before my parents return from their trip. We can do weekdays, if you prefer, so as not to intrude on your weekends with Nick."

Jean thought, "Sure. Let me get back to you tomorrow with the dates. It will be nice to have a vacation even if it is a working one."

As the ladies were getting up to leave for water aerobics, the bell rang as the door opened and Nick walked inside. Jean was very surprised but tried not to show it. "Hi, this is a surprise," she said as Nick walked over to give her a brief kiss. They tried not to be overly expressive of their affection in public.

"I thought you wouldn't be here today since the Attic is closed. I thought you would be in the pool by now."

Jean's brows creased, "So I take it you aren't here to see me then."

Nick kind of blushed while he answered, "Actually, I wanted to talk to Fannie about a matter."

Tension was growing slightly, Jean said, "You know she is going to tell me anyway, so do you want me to stay to hear it firsthand?"

Nick, trying to make light of the situation, laughed in a fake way, "This will give you something to talk about later."

Heading out the door so Fannie and Nick could be alone, Jean paused, "I take it you finally got ballistics back on that unidentified dead body found a few weeks ago on the beach." Jean then turned and proceeded out the door.

Nick said with expression, "Damn, I hate it when she does that!"

Fannie was truly in the dark so asked, "Does what?"

Nick confided in Fannie, "I don't talk about my cases with Jean. I used to, but when I would come up with a great idea after a date or weekend with Jean, they figured out that she might be helping. I was called in and read the riot act by the chief. I told him that I didn't tell Jean everything, that she reads the papers and is just good at figuring things out. I was told not to tell her anything or confirm anything she said. I haven't. Somehow she can still figure it out."

Fannie, after years with Jean, knew how she was able to guess, "Tell me about it. One time, I told her I did something that she wouldn't like and she guessed that I got a tattoo, just out of the blue. Now who would guess that? I said yes. Then she just said 'on your bottom right?' It's like she can see through people."

Nick was laughing for real now, "I better get to my questions before I find out more information that I don't really want to know. Fannie, I need to ask you some questions about the gun you found in the box that you got at the auction. A .45 colt is not totally rare but not in everyone's gun case. Did anyone else bid on that box at the auction? Did you see anyone watching or acting suspicious at the auction? Just tell me in your own words about the bidding, please."

Fannie thought, "There were very few people bidding. I think if the western style outfit was on top that more people would have bid on it, but it was buried under some junky looking items. It was a nice surprise to see something that could actually sell. A lot of people were bidding on the furniture and drapes. I heard comments that made me think some of the bidders also had secondhand stores. I know two or three of the people came from shops on James Street close to downtown in the city. I can write down their names and store names for you if you like. This type of business is like a small community; even if we aren't friends, we know each other. Costumes have a very limited appeal so dealers didn't bid on those. There were a couple of younger girls there from Wayne High School that bought a couple of boxes, but they dug through to find ones that worked for their upcoming play this year. I didn't see them touch the box with the guns in them. There was this ugly plaid suit on top, next were tacky tourist outfits, so everyone looked at it and walked away. I figure there are plenty of people with bad taste out there, and for five dollars a box, why not try? At the end, after I carried the last box to the van, this middle-aged, really skinny, well-dressed woman came rushing in. She asked how it was going and if everything sold. I take it from the people working the auction that she was a big shot at the theatre. When they said everything sold and it was over, she said that was good and apologized for being late. I don't think she was sincerely sorry about being late or wanting to help with the auction. She looked around the empty room and headed down the hall."

Nick, through his questioning, obtained an exact description of the woman in charge, the business card of the people conducting the auction, the names of the other antique dealers complete with addresses and descriptions and first names of the high school students. Fannie was an observant person also. Now the questioning turned to the gun. "Who was here when the gun was discovered and who knows of its existence?"

Fannie looked surprised, "So Jean was right, it is about the gun. Is it the murder victim on the beach?"

Nick turned serious, "I'm not kidding about the boss being angry. I could lose my job."

Fannie felt sorry for Nick, "I won't even discuss this interview with Jean if that helps. She will probably trick me into it but I will try. Why don't you just tell her what happened with your boss? She would understand."

Nick looked sad, "Pride, I guess."

Fannie tried to be helpful, "I don't like guns. I freaked out when I saw it. I was not surprised to know Jean knew a lot about the gun but was shocked that Priscilla knew how to check to see if it was loaded. Belinda, Eve, Priscilla, Jo and Jean were here helping me with the boxes and no one was in the store. The six of us knew it was in the desk drawer and where the key was. To my knowledge, only you, Jean and I know the gun was taken. I don't know if Jean has told anyone."

Nick, on a long shot, asked, "Has anyone that you saw at the auction visited the store since the gun arrived?"

Fannie took time for a serious review, "Not that I know of, and I don't remember being out and letting anyone else run the store since then."

Nick thanked her for her time. Of course she knew how to get in touch with him if she thought of anything else. Fannie gave him a hug, promising him she would continue to think about it and not say anything to Jean.

Jean stopped by after the water workout thinking Fannie would tell her everything. Fannie did tell Jean one thing but not what Jean expected. "Jean, Nick is worried about losing his job. They are accusing him of telling too much to someone not in the department."

Jean looked surprised, "He doesn't tell me things. I can just figure it out."

Fannie was serious when she said, "Well, stop it."

Chapter 15 – Avoiding the Truth

On Tuesday night, Belinda and Jean loaded the van and packed the items they might need, like a hammer, picture hanging material, a ladder and more. They headed to the winter home of Belinda's parents on Wednesday. It was the middle of the morning when they arrived at the art show. "Having a van could be dangerous," said Jean, "You have no excuse to stop shopping since we have so much room to put our purchases."

"Thanks for shopping with me, Jean. I know shopping is not your favorite thing," said Belinda sincerely.

Jean smiled but didn't deny the statement, "I'm glad you got the paint samples and pictures of the room. It sure helps to know that we are making the right choices."

The plan was to make a quick round of the booths to see what was available, then do the selections and paint comparisons on anything that stood out as being a possibility for the room. It was going to be a long day in the warm sun but there was a nice breeze making the day most pleasant. "At least it is great weather," Belinda said brightly, "Let me buy some drinks since you're doing me the favor of coming along on this venture." Walking away from the concession stand, Belinda put her hand out to stop Jean. "Look over there," she said. "Isn't that Patty? She is crying, well actually sobbing. We can't just walk away." Belinda went to the stressed girl and put her arm around her. "Are you ok?"

Patty looked up but didn't try to smile. "Yes, I'm alright, just hurt and sad."

Belinda continued to try to comfort her, "I can see that. Do you want to talk? Can I get you something to drink?"

Patty held up her drink as an answer to the question. "I had a very bad argument with my grandfather and grandmother. They asked me to come home alone this weekend. You know, without Richard. After dinner, they took me into the office and tried to show me what they considered proof that Richard was just using me. I know he loves me and they are wrong. They told me that since I wouldn't listen, they would have to prove it to me. I just tried to purchase a painting that I think would be perfect for our new home, and my trust account credit card was denied. I was so embarrassed. I called the company and was told the card is temporarily suspended. I called and talked to my grandfather. He said that if Richard and I were willing to live on our salaries for a long number of years, that would prove to them that Richard is with me for loving me and not love of my money. They said they might eventually allow me access to the trust fund if they felt Richard was sincere in his love. The trust specified charities that my parents wanted the money to go to if it didn't go to me. My grandparents might give my money away. That provision was in the trust in case we died at the same time, not to be used to control and manipulate me. I'm mad, angry, hurt and a little scared."

Belinda looked surprised, "Scared of what? Are you afraid Richard will leave you?"

"Yes. Not because Richard doesn't love me, he does, but because he is sensitive. I'm afraid he will take this rejection by my family personally and very hard. I'm also scared because even though I have a good job, I certainly don't earn the type of money I'm used to living on. My salary is used for travel, parties or clothes. My living expenses have always been billed to the trust fund. I don't know if I can adjust to a lesser lifestyle. I'm being made to choose between my comfortable living arrangement and the man I love. Richard is the only man to ever pay attention to me. He didn't know how rich I was when we first met and yet he poured out his heart to me immediately. I guess I will just have to prove them wrong and stay with Richard. When they see Richard is still just as dedicated to me as ever, maybe they will let me have access to the money again. I don't know if I should tell Richard the truth or pretend it is my idea that we have a struggling newlywed lifestyle for the sake of bonding."

Belinda nodded, "I do think being honest is a good thing in a relationship but I can see where that might cause a rift between Richard and your grandparents that might not be easy to overcome. You do have a hard decision to make, and while I'm glad to listen and be there for you as a friend, no one can decide your path but you. I know your grandparents well and know how much they love you so I'm sure this isn't to hurt you but to help you grow."

A snort came out of Patty, "I wish I could believe that but right now I'm too hurt to think you are right. I do appreciate you talking to me. You're very understanding, especially considering that your friend Priscilla is so involved. Thank you for talking with me. While you didn't say anything to form my opinion, after this open discussion, I'm going to pretend it was my idea. Once they see Richard's love for me, poor or rich, they will reinstate the money and he will never know their doubts about him."

As Patty walked away, Jean who listened but remained silent the whole conversation said, "She will find out the truth now. She is going to be so hurt when it comes out."

Belinda being the optimist said, "Maybe we are wrong. Maybe he really does love her and it will work out."

Jean, turned to look at her friend like she just grew horns and a tail, refused to comment. "Let's get back to our task before it gets any later."

"My dad is more of the structure type guy who likes angles and shapes in a picture, while my mom and I would choose the French impressionism painting. I know he won't like them. I want to pick something they both like, not just what she wants and he tolerates because he is too nice to say anything." Jean and Belinda turned to each other and both said at the same time, "Booth #17." They selected this very large painting with what looked like black lines filled with colors in the spaces between the lines. The artist made the colors spill over so it looked three-dimensional, like the colors lifted off the canvas spilling over the black. At booth #32, there was metal artwork of three sailing ships in black. Jean selected some planters that hung on the wall with greenery and flowers to help soften the dramatic larger pieces. With their shopping done, they headed to the house.

Chapter 16 – Barb's Visit

The next morning, Belinda and Jean got up to work on the finishing touches of the room. "We really needed Fannie for this. She is the artist, not me," Jean professed.

Belinda smiled, "We can do this just fine. Fannie couldn't get away for enough days to come but she kept telling me hints of what to do. We can always do a video and pictures to send for her approval or recommendations."

Jean was very pleased with the picture and wall hanging. "Why does your mother leave an undecorated wreath and Christmas tree out all year?"

Belinda explained, "She says if she decorates them now, it won't be special for Christmas. I guess you are going to put them into storage How about we leave them out then ask them when they arrive?"

Jean was firm, "If you surprise them with the perfect room, it needs to have everything in place exactly like you want it. We can bring out the wreath and tree if they insist but if they see the room without them, they can get a better idea of why they shouldn't be here. They are just in the closet three feet away. Also, it helps keep down the dust not to have them sitting around."

Jean was on a roll now, "This bar set we got from Fannie has the wrong color at the bottom and it looks terrible. We need to paint it black to make the ships and picture stand out better. I saw black spray paint out in the garage. Can you use the paint?"

Belinda looked nervous, "Yes. I brought it to paint the lamp. My nephew did the painting and I'm not sure if we can do it as good."

Jean again looked over in a negative way, "Do you really think we can't do it right? Of course we can. I didn't bring any paint clothes. Did you bring some or have some around the house we can use?"

Belinda shook her head no. By this time, Jean had the bar outside on a drop cloth in the yard and was sanding away the old paint. After cleaning off all the dust and sand, Jean entered the garage and walked in the closet. She emerged with a black, fifty-gallon trash bag over her underwear and was headed back outside.

Belinda was laughing so hard she had to sit down, "What are you doing? You aren't going outside like that, are you?"

MIA TENROC

Jean gave a grin, "I will never see any of these people again so what do I care if they see me wearing a trash bag? I'm not going to ruin my clothes by getting paint on them. I'm not exposing anything so we shouldn't get arrested." Jean was in the yard painting when she looked up and out came Belinda wearing an equally fashionable outfit of a black bag.

Belinda was taking pictures of Jean and the furniture. "I heard a honk before I came out. Did someone you know come by?"

Jean laughing said, "No, I didn't know the person, but with one look at me, he was laughing so hard, I think he hit his head on the horn of the car. You do realize in the future this might appear in one of my books?"

Belinda looked serious as she said, "I certainly hope so. I would hate to think we got all dressed up for nothing."

Right then, a Mercedes turned into the driveway and Barb, Patty's grandmother, got out. "Act natural like we wear trash bags every day," Jean whispered. Belinda walked over with a smile on her face while extending her hand to greet Barb.

Barb looked the ladies up and down and asked, "Did I catch you at a bad time?"

Jean introduced herself, "No, we just put on the last coat of paint and it needs to dry, so this is good timing. Would you like to go inside and have some tea?"

Barb accepted, "Are you sure you have a few minutes?"

Both Belinda and Jean nodded yes as Jean put on the kettle. "Hope you have the time because tea is so much better brewed instead of microwaved."

Barb relaxed a little thinking maybe they weren't too weird after all. At least they knew proper tea etiquette. "I feel silly talking to you about this and I do hope you won't let a word get back to my husband. You ladies know all the parties involved with this man who is dating our granddaughter. Last night, we cut her off her money she receives monthly. My husband tried to tell her that this man is just using her and she wouldn't listen. Alex makes all the decisions, and while I agree with him about this man that Patty is mixed up with being no good, do you think we are doing the right thing?"

Tears started to flow and again it was Belinda trying to be comforting, "Everyone has to do what they think is best. I would never judge you for your decision." They continued their conversation with Jean silently looking on.

Finally, Jean could be silent no longer, "Look, the majority of people live on what Patty makes and I think it is a good idea to teach a child to be self-supporting. It isn't like you are putting her on the street. She is making a decision and now she is going to live with her choices. I think that is a good thing. Nothing you did or said was so horrible that it creates a big division. I think you did the right thing and if he really does love Patty, then you can welcome them back once you're sure."

Barb got up to leave and gave each a hug. "Thank you so much for talking with me. I feel much better."

After Barb pulled away, Belinda turned to Jean showing how upset she was, "What did you do? You shouldn't have given an opinion!"

Jean calmly said, "She wanted our opinion so I gave it to her. She felt better afterwards. I'm proud of myself for not telling my real opinion of the jerk. At least I just said the right things to support her and not get myself sued for slander."

Chapter 17 – At the Lawyer's Office

The next morning, Jean and Belinda were working on the final staging of the party room when they heard a car pull into the driveway. Barb entered the garage and into the party room where they were working. She couldn't help the explanation of surprise that escaped her mouth upon seeing the beautiful completed work. "Now I understand how those people on the home improvement shows feel when they see their remodeled house completed. I didn't have the vision to see how exquisite this room could become," she said.

Belinda smiled, "Are you coming to the party tomorrow for my parent's 65th wedding anniversary?"

"I wouldn't miss it," said Barb.

"You look so much happier today," stated Jean. "Are you feeling better about everything?"

Barb's smile went away, "Yes, I do feel better. Your words convinced me that my husband wants to do the right thing. I was born into a wealthy family and married into equal wealth so I don't know or understand what my wonderful Patty will be going through. But I do need to know that her new relationship is the right thing."

Jean gave a look to Belinda that said 'I told you so', while she was speaking to Barb, "Barb, let me assure you that I never had much in life, especially when I was younger, and I made it through just fine. In fact, I feel that the lessons and hard times in life made me a better person."

Barb came over and extended her hand to Jean, "I have a favor to ask. I need to go to the attorney's office today to sign some paperwork. Would you come with me? We can make it a fun day of going to lunch then shopping if you like?"

Belinda, needing Jean's help, spoke up, "We will be glad to go with you to the law office and lunch but then we need to get back here to finish the preparations for the party."

Jean agreed, "The preparing does includes some shopping. Do you want to help?"

Barb said, "I think that would be the perfect distraction from my worry over Patty. Thank you for including me. I would love to join you."

Belinda and Jean sat in the reception room of the law firm with Barb when the door opened and the secretary escorted the current customer out. Jean's eyes went wide with the sight of Helen ReSol walking out the door. Barb stood and walked over to give Helen a socially polite hug, "So good to see you, Helen. I didn't know you used Mr. Craft's services."

Helen, taken very off guard especially at the presence of Jean, spoke to Barb, "You recommended his services so highly in the past that my husband and I have moved a part of our business here."

Belinda and Jean stood and moved over with Barb but they, of course, were not hug worthy. Jean's real intention was to try to see what paperwork was in Helen's arms.

There was a folder sticking from the top of the designer bag Helen carried that had the word "Will" on it. Jean, working with the legal profession for years, knew that attorneys used the cover on the last Will and Testament of people to protect the contents.

Helen was staring in a very unpleasant way at Jean as she looked up from the paper. Barb, not noticing the exchange, continued talking, "Belinda's parents are returning from Europe tomorrow and we are having a surprise 65th wedding anniversary for them. Are you planning to come?"

Helen, trying to sound natural most unsuccessfully, replied, "I wasn't invited! We wouldn't be attending anyway. My husband prefers to stay home more lately. He works so hard and is tired after a long day so we like our quiet and alone time."

Belinda interjected, trying to smooth things over cheerfully, "The ReSol family doesn't know my parents so the lack of invitation wasn't intended to be an insult, but instead to not burden them unnecessarily with a social event they probably wouldn't want to attend."

The secretary interrupted by saying, "Mr. Craft will see you now."

"So nice to see you, Barb," Helen said as she walked out the door escaping from the undesirable people remaining in the room.

Standing by the windows looking outside and out of hearing range of the receptionist, Belinda spoke to Jean, "I would never invite her anywhere. I'm glad my parents haven't been exposed to such a rude person. She really seems to hate you for some reason, Jean. What did you ever do to her?"

Right then, Jean's phone rang. "It's Fannie," she whispered to Belinda. "Yeah, that's fine. No, don't worry about it. See you tonight."

Belinda turned to Jean, "What do you mean see you tonight? You are supposed to stay here and help with my parent's party."

"I will stay and help get everything ready today and leave to go up after dinner. Fannie needs her van back for some deliveries and pickups tomorrow. It was nice of her to loan it to us so I don't want to take advantage of her. Steve is coming down in the morning so you will have his car to get back to Abletown. Your parents' cars are here for you to use until he arrives. There will be about a hundred people at the party so I won't be missed."

Belinda turned from watching Helen getting in her car, "Did you ever notice how much Fannie and Helen look like from the back? They are about the same height, age, curvy body and blonde hair. They don't look at all alike from the front. Fannie is a natural blonde, and with those black eyebrows, it is easy to see Helen should have dark hair. This is the first time I ever thought about the similarities."

Chapter 18 – At the Playhouse

Nick and his partner, Janice, headed to the theatre venue on a fishing expedition. They had no reason to believe this lovely facility of art and culture had anything to do with the dead body on the beach except for a gut instinct by Nick.

The middle-aged, really skinny, well-dressed woman turned out to be the director, Miriam Highland. "I always appreciate the law enforcement agency and their hard work but I don't understand what you are here for."

Nick tried to explain. "We found a body on the beach and wondered if you knew of anyone that was missing that fits the description: female, late twenties or early thirties, 5'4", about 138 pounds, brown hair."

Ms. Highland looked confused, "I think that description fits a lot of people. Do you have a picture?

I still don't know why you are asking me. No, I don't know anyone missing."

Nick pressed on, "I just wondered and see no harm in asking. The young lady deserves justice. I don't have a photo and the face is missing."

Ms. Highland looked down her nose at the detectives, "Did you lose it too?"

Nick could feel his blood pressure rising, "It was eaten away by the wildlife in the water, after it was shot." He intended to shock to get her attention, "Would it be ok for us to ask around the staff here to see if they know of anyone?"

Janice decided to have a try at the interview, "There was a gun sold by this theatre that is the same caliber as the bullet that killed this woman."

"This theatre doesn't sell guns! What you are saying makes no sense at all." Miriam tried to square her shoulders to look superior and tough.

Janice said, "I think the fact that a gun was in a box that came from this venue is cause to at least permit our asking questions here. If you don't agree, I will be forced to ask a judge for permission based on your lack of cooperation."

Nick had to laugh. Janice didn't even want to come here and her instant dislike of Miriam Highland was enough to jump into the investigation with a new enthusiasm.

"There are no employees to ask! I'm the only full-time employee and Brittney, our part-time employee, just started two weeks ago."

Nick looked confused, "How can a theatre group have so few employees?"

Miriam was starting to get agitated, "If you must know, this is how the company works. There were three rich families in the area that felt a need to add a little culture to this community. There are six on the board of directors, either members of those families or their appointed representative. I do almost all the running of the playhouse. The board decides the plays we will do. I take care of getting all the approvals and hiring the actors. I am also the accountant for this operation. I work with the university professor that teaches media jobs like lights and sound. The school provides students to act as director, the lights person and sound tech for each production. It is a different group each time because working with us for a month or one production of a play is a school credit. It is not a paid position. The professor and I oversee their work to make sure it meets our standard and to make sure they are handling their duties correctly. We work with a company called Visual Beauty. They take care of the set and staging for each production but it isn't enough work to hire someone full-time. They also stage local homes that are being sold and help with other acting groups. Besides being paid for the work, they get free advertising in the programs. Our part-time worker acts as receptionist from 10:00 to 2:00 each day. Her duties include handling ticket request for individual sale, making sure we have volunteers to usher and occasionally calling local businesses for advertising. I pick up on anything she didn't get done and handle the tickets for the members of the theatre."

Janice, needing some clarification, asked, "Do you have actors you normally use regularly?"

Miriam responded, "No, I seldom use the same actors because someone might think of them based on another role they did, so I prefer fresh faces. I do use some local actors more than once in a year but never in back-to-back productions."

Janice continued, "Have you had a turnover on the part-time position recently?"

Miriam stopped trying to hide her anger, "Yes, a few different girls have had the job. I usually hire from a local temp agency so they can get insurance through the agency. It costs a little more but gives us discounts because without other employees, our obligation by state and federal government changes. We are non-profit, so keeping overhead low is very important. After the last temp was caught stealing some credit card information, which was reported to the police, the board decided it was best to have our own employee. Brittney is the granddaughter of one of the founders. You really have taken up so much of my time and for no reason. This conversation is over so I will walk you to the door."

The dismissal didn't set well with the two detectives. In the car, Nick said, "I still think something is going on with her. I think we should check with the staging company. If that is a dead end, then we can drop this but I just can't keep from thinking of the real gun being sold from here as important to some murder, even if it isn't ours."

Chapter 19 – Judith Lane

Visual Beauty was a warehouse with only one car parked outside. An opening large enough for a truck to enter was on the south end. The detectives entered with Nick calling out, "Hello." A man about 5 foot 10 inches, 185 pounds, about 50 years of age walked towards them wiping his hands on a rag which he stuffed into his tool belt when done.

"Art Parker, what can I do for you?" he said as an introduction.

"Nicholas Noble and my partner, Janice Hoover, we are detectives on the police force," said Nick. They held out their badges.

Art was a little surprised, "I've never talked to a real life detective before. I never really talked to the police except for a couple of traffic stops." A woman entered the warehouse from a little office in the corner.

"This is my wife, Nora. We have police detectives here, Mr. Noble and Ms. Hoover. What can we do for you?"

Nick started the questioning, "We have the body of a woman that should have been reported missing. We are trying to discover her identity." Nick described the body.

Art was rubbing his head, "Always sad for the loss of such a young life, but why are you here talking with us?"

Janice answered, "We wondered if anyone fitting that description ever worked at or acted with the theatre group."

Nora looked like a light came on, "About two or three months ago, there was a receptionist that fit that description named Judith Lane. She was a really sweet girl and very quiet. She certainly wasn't the party type. One day, she just wasn't working there. I inquired about Judith and Ms. Highland said she had a family emergency and moved home. Something about her mother being ill, I think."

"Do you know where her family lived?" asked Nick.

"No, I don't know where she was from," Nora answered.

"Do you know if she had any friends, boyfriends, hangout spots?" Janice asked.

Nora thought, "We didn't really talk that much. I don't recall her mentioning anyone."

Art then added to the conversation, "I took her home a couple of times. She lived on Nottingham Road. Turn right out of here, go about a mile and Nottingham is on the right. I don't remember the number but it was a four unit building on the right, second from the main road. It's the only unit type building there so you can't miss it."

Janice tried to ask in an innocent way, "It seems strange Miriam Highland didn't remember her during our interview. I mean since they worked together."

Nora's expression showed her disdain, "Miriam Highland never thinks of anyone but herself. She looks down her nose at everyone and never listens when they talk, like she is too good to mess with the little people. I'm not surprised she wouldn't remember or think of Judith. She only speaks to people when she wants them to do something for her then forgets them."

"Not a fan, I take it," said Nick with a smile. "Thank you for your help and time. Have a good day."

Back in the car, Nick consulted with Janice, "Continue our inquires, I presume? We may or may not be going anywhere with this but it sure won't hurt to follow up."

Janice agreed, "I think Miriam Highland is hiding something so let's find out what."

They had no trouble finding the apartment building and knocked on the door that was marked owner. An elderly gentleman, Bob Cross, opened the door and welcomed them inside.

"Judith," Bob said with a smile, "Really sweet girl, quiet, no visitors that I can remember. I liked her but she sure did leave in an odd way."

"What do you mean?" asked Nick.

"She was behind on her rent. I let it go because she was such a good tenant. I knew she would pay me when she could. She worked for the theatre group part-time and they didn't pay much. She was looking for other work and promised to pay as soon as she had more income. I believed her. It's hard to find good tenants so I was willing to work with her. One day, she just never came home. She just left all her stuff. I asked at the theatre if they had seen her and they just said no, that she walked out on them too."

Janice, trying not to appear eager, asked, "Who did you talk to at the theatre?"

Bob thought, "I don't remember the name but some skinny, nasty woman. She didn't care about Judith, only that work needed to be done."

Nick inquired, "Do you know where she lived before she came here? Do you know where her family lives?"

Bob shook his head, "No family, she said both her parents died when she was 18. She lived with her grandmother until she passed. Maybe that's why I was so willing to work with her. She had no one to go to and nowhere to go."

"What happened to her possessions?" asked Nick.

"The furniture I gave to a charity that was willing to pick up. I boxed up her personal items and clothes. They are in the shed out back. I just threw away the food and anything that would spoil. You can have what's in the shed if you like."

Janice inquired about a car.

Bob pulled out a paper from a file and provided them a make, model and plate number.

The boxes were placed in the trunk of Nick's car. The detectives thanked Bob for his time and help. They gave him a business card with the number to call in case he thought of something further.

As they drove away, Janice was already calling to have a check run on the license number of the car.

Chapter 20 – Viking Heir

Priscilla was in her apartment with her grandsons. Craig was bouncing off the walls with energy and Priscilla was having a hard time keeping him quiet. "Let's go to the pool," Craig shouted.

"I don't want to go outside," Jerry insisted.

Priscilla knocked on Jean's door. "Help!"

Jean smiled, "What's going on?"

Priscilla answered, "The boys have the day off school. My daughter and her attorney are meeting with the other side to discuss the property settlement agreement. I brought the boys here because they love to swim and I thought it would be a good distraction. Craig wants to go to the pool but Jerry is depressed and refuses to go outside. He is just sitting and playing games on the computer. Could you keep an eye on him while I take Craig out? You don't have to come to my apartment but just leave the doors open and if Jerry needs anything, he can come over."

"Glad to help," said Jean.

After Priscilla and Craig left, Jean went into Priscilla's apartment. "How are you doing?" she inquired. Jerry wouldn't reply so Jean persisted. "What is so bad? Do you want to talk?"

"No!" shouted Jerry.

"Did you go to the convention yesterday? Anyone who loves video games and animes would have been there." Jean was trying to reach common ground.

Jerry looked up with a tear in his eye. "My friends offered to let me go with them and were even going to pay my way but my dad refused to let me go. He said it was his time and I had to do what he wanted. We sat around the house all day doing nothing. My friends will all be talking about it tomorrow and I will be left out. I wanted to go so bad and it's only once a year so now I have to wait until next year for the fun. I'm so mad at my dad. Mom tried to talk to him and explain it was important. She even offered to give up her time next weekend but the jerk wouldn't let me go. He hates me! Nothing I do or say is good enough. He doesn't want me to be happy." Jean looked shocked. Jerry continued, "Don't give me a lecture about I shouldn't feel this way. I do!"

Jean said, "Oh, no! I have to say I'm in total agreement with you." Now it was Jerry's turn to be surprised. "I think that was horrible. I don't see how any man could do that to his son. I think he should have let you go and I think he should have asked to go with you."

"Did you go to the convention?" Jerry asked.

Jean smiled, "To be honest, my son would never have wanted me to go with him. Besides, I'm not into gaming and that style of movies but that doesn't mean I don't understand the importance of the event. Will you trust me enough to go on a ride somewhere that I think will really make you happy? It isn't near as good as the convention but at least it will be somewhere you will enjoy."

Jerry agreed to go. After all, Jean did seem to understand why he was upset. She didn't say those stupid things like you can go next year or it was only a convention. Jean and Jerry stopped by the pool to let Priscilla know they would be gone a couple of hours. Priscilla was just grateful that Jerry seemed to be responding so she didn't ask questions.

They drove to town and pulled into the parking lot of Viking Heir Gaming and Comics. Jerry jumped out of the car. "This is so cool!" They walked inside and the workers were all in costumes. To the right was an area to play games while you had a drink or snacks. To the left was the register and straight ahead was a throne. A man sat dressed in Viking attire. Customers would walk up to him to discuss games, movies or comics they were considering purchasing from the huge store supply that was spread out from the cashier to the back of the store. "Where are your horns?" asked Jerry.

The man, about 30 old with long hair, laughed, "Real Vikings didn't wear horns. That was Hollywood's idea of the costume."

"Are you a real Viking?" asked Jerry as he smiled with happiness at this adventure.

"Yes," explained Alan.

Jean explained, "Alan is my son. His wife is over at the register dressed in the Black Widow costume from the Avenger series. This is their store." Jean turned to her son, "Alan, this is Jerry, Priscilla's grandson. Can you believe his father didn't permit him to go to the convention this weekend?"

"WHAT! No man should ever do that." Alan was sincere in his expression.

Jerry was laughing, "It is so nice to be understood."

Jean spoke to Alan so Jerry couldn't hear. Alan motioned another employee to come over and sit on the throne. Alan put his arm around Jerry and said, "Let's go play a game in that glass enclosed office in the corner. You can pick the game."

Jerry was quickly looking through the selection, chose one and headed to the office. "Your son is so cool. Is he really a Viking?"

Jean smiled, "We are descended from Vikings. We have never lived nor practiced that lifestyle, but that is why the store is named Viking Heir."

Jean went off to the gaming section and left the two young men alone to play their game.

After a long discussion about the game they were playing, which included the game path and adversaries, Alan began asking questions about Jerry. What kind of games and movies did Jerry like? Who was Jerry's favorite superhero? Did Jerry like Marvel? Alan showed Jerry a picture of him with Stan Lee. Alan brought the conversation to a more personal level. How did Jerry do in school? What are Jerry's hopes and dreams?

Jerry said, "No one has ever asked me about what I like so much. It is so great of you to take time to hang out with me. I don't know that I'm good enough to do anything. I especially can't imagine owning such a cool store."

Alan then told his history, "I was an unhappy college professor. Most people would think that teaching college was being successful but it doesn't matter how much you earn or what titles you have if you are not happy with your work. I'm doing what I love. I wouldn't consider all those years in chemistry a waste but I didn't want to give it any more of my time. I believe you should follow your dream even if people think you're crazy."

"Did your Mom and Dad support your dream of running this store?" Jerry really wanted to know. He wasn't just making conversation.

"I never knew my father and that is ok because you should love and value what you have, not worrying about what is missing from your life. I have a great mom. Mom cared if I was happy and wanted me to follow my dream. She even gave me her house to live in so I could afford the starting costs of the store," Alan said with appreciation.

"You don't care that your dad wasn't around?" Jerry asked in a sad way.

Alan was firm, "No. Even if he was around and even if no one approved of my career change, I would have done it anyway. I do believe in right and wrong. I would never do anything I felt was bad but there is nothing wrong with enjoying my life the way it is. You don't need other people's approval to feel you are worthy. You only need to be proud of yourself to know you are doing the right thing. You need to remember, too, that there are some people that will never give you their approval. Be kind, be respectful but be true to yourself. Don't let someone else drag you down. I think you are a nice young man. It sounds like you are doing great in school. I know about your parents and the divorce. You have to stay focused on yourself and your future and not let their negativity bring you down."

Jerry gave Alan a hug, "Thank you. Can I talk to you again sometime?"

Alan said, "Sure. I need to get back to work. Why don't you take that game home with you? Maybe make up for what you missed yesterday."

Jerry was smiling and dancing as they walked to the car. Jean received a hug before Jerry walked around to get in the passenger side.

At home, Priscilla couldn't believe the change in Jerry. Jerry offered to play the game with Craig as he went into the same explanation that Alan had given him. Priscilla had tears in her eyes as Jean received another hug.

Chapter 21 – The Divorce

Priscilla turned to Jean, "I don't know how the attorney got such a quick court date for the divorce but I'm glad they did, it will be nice to get it over with. Richard hasn't given Kathy a dime of child support since he left so now he will be forced to. He tried to get out of paying any since the dance studio fired him but there isn't any reason he can't work another job. He's not that great of a dancer so he should try to find another profession."

Belinda offered to stay with the boys so Jean could go to court with Kathy and Priscilla to be their emotional support. Richard, accompanied by Patty, his parents and their attorney, entered the court. Richard's attorney, Vic Story, walked over to Jean as she stood up to shake hands. "Do you want to have lunch after the trial?" he asked.

Priscilla and Kathy both turned with open mouths at Jean being friendly with the opposition as she accepted the offer. "What are you doing?" Priscilla demanded.

Jean assured them, "Vic was one of my customers when I was in the title business. We are old friends. Besides, you never know what you might learn in a nice conversation over lunch."

The ReSol party didn't hear what was said but Helen shot dirty looks at Jean as Patty waved hi to Jean behind Helen's back.

The case only took minutes to be completed. The parties went to the bench. Did both agree to the terms of the property settlement? Yes. Did both complete the required course in parenting as a divorced parent? Yes. Did anyone have any comments or questions? No. A hit of the gavel and it was done.

Kathy and Priscilla went to Kathy's house while Jean went to the diner across the street. Vic arrived and they greeted each other again. "What are you doing working on a divorce case?" inquired Jean.

Vic laughed, "I do try to avoid them. In fact, I can't stand them. I do all the legal work for the ReSol family. Charles would never go to another attorney. He is a client and a good friend. I would never refuse to do work for him. Since divorce isn't my specialty, I did get assistance from another attorney in the firm to make sure I did it right. I probably said more than I should but that's why I accepted a divorce case. I take it you are on the other side."

"Priscilla makes my best friend list. I will be honest and say I can't stand the ReSols, especially Helen and Richard. Charles actually seems very nice. You didn't tell me anything I didn't already know as far as you representing Charles ReSol on his real estate transactions. I did your title work and remembered his name on a few of the orders you placed. Now that we have stated which camp we are in, why don't we talk about more pleasant things?"

A pleasant conversation proceeded about the real estate market and mutual friends but Jean couldn't stop thinking to herself that if Vic did all the ReSol business, why was Helen coming out of the office of Mr. Craft?

Chapter 22 – Over Before It Began

It was Richard's evening with the boys but at the last minute he called to cancel. "I need to go out to celebrate my freedom tonight with Princess P. I'll get the kids another time."

Jean offered to take Kathy and Priscilla out to celebrate so they wouldn't be sitting home alone after the emotionally draining day. Belinda was going as a thank you for staying with the boys. They were ready to walk out the door as soon as the boys left, so now it was time to change their plans. "I can't go out and leave the boys," said Kathy. "What a jerk. He doesn't care about anyone but himself. Why don't the three of you go out without me?"

"The boys seem a little down too. Do you think they would want to join us?" suggested Belinda.

Priscilla made a face, "We are going to the pub on the boat dock. The boys can't go in there."

Belinda suggested, "We could eat outside, not in the bar. The customers come by boats as well as cars. Maybe the boys would enjoy seeing the boats and airboats."

Jean made a call, "Alan to the rescue again. Besides, it really helped Jerry after his last visit with Alan. It might be the best thing for them to do something fun that they like. Alan promised pizza for dinner then planned to take them back to the store for a gaming competition."

Kathy was worried, "That is fine for Jerry but does Alan have any clue how active Craig is? It might be too much."

Jean responded, "Alan has a whole staff to help run after Craig. His wife is great with kids. They have games for his age group in the store. Besides, what could be better than a free run of the store?"

Kathy called the boys from their room. "You father isn't coming to get you. You have three choices. One is to stay home and we can rent a movie. Two is going out to eat with us at the docks. I think it would be ok if we ate outside. The third is going to Viking Heir for an evening of gaming."

The boys' choice was obvious as they cheered and jumped around the room. Kathy told Jerry, "You need to help keep an eye on Craig and not let him get into anything."

"I promise! Craig, wait until you see this place! It's like going to heaven!" Jerry's excitement couldn't be contained.

They dropped the boys off at the store. Jean announced, "I'm driving and buying, so feel free to drink all you like. This is a celebration."

"I can't drink because of my medication," said Kathy.

"One is my limit or you will carry me out. You know that," said Priscilla.

Jean glanced over at Belinda who was hiding her smile. She promised. "Don't worry, I will make up for them."

When they walked into the bar, Jean spotted Josephine walking from the restroom to the table in the corner that was hidden by the bar. Michael and Eve were sitting at a table also. "I didn't know you were coming tonight."

Michael replied, "Jo felt the need to see where I left the frogs."

"And you? Did you have a concern for the frogs?" Jean asked Eve.

Eve acted indignant, "No, I could care less about the frogs but needed a night out. Linda is driving me crazy."

The next table was open so the ladies sat down. They were separated but could join each other's conversations if desired.

The meal was proceeding with good food, drink, and pleasant conversation when a loud annoying voice on the other side of the bar announced, "Let's celebrate! I'm free of the ball and chain forever!"

Josephine stood and walked a couple of steps to confirm the loud mouth fool was none other than Richard ReSol. Richard was sitting at the bar. "Would you like food with that drink?" asked the bartender.

"No, my new physical and financial partner is on the way to pay for my party and later give me pleasure. I better wait until she arrives."

The group stayed hidden from Richard's sight and ate in silence. It was almost 30 minutes before Patty walked into the bar. "I was worried about my Princess. I missed you so much. It is so good to see you," Richard said as he leaned in for his kiss.

Patty slapped his face. "My grandparents are right. You don't care about me. You just want my money!" The whole bar went quiet. While people didn't stare at the couple, all ears were waiting to hear what would occur next, especially the ladies at the table.

Richard jumped up and put his arms around Patty, "My sweet Patty, my beautiful princess. Don't act like that. Please sit down and have a drink and tell me what happened. I love you. I left my wife for you. Things were fine in court. Please talk to me."

Patty started crying. "I went to a shower for a friend. They were laughing about a dance instructor who made a pass at Lydia and professed his love to her.

Then this same man told Pamela he loved her and tried to get her to marry him. I looked at the pictures on their phones and it was you! They confirmed you are nothing but a gold digger looking for your next victim and it is me! How could I have been so stupid to believe you cared? I would give you back your engagement ring but I paid for it, not you. I never want to see you again. I hate you and want you out of my life forever."

Patty ran out of the bar with Richard running behind her. Patty made it to her airboat and she was trying to start it. She pushed Richard away with an emergency oar that is kept on the boat. He fell off the dock into the water below. He swam to shore at the point where the walking trail from the restaurant came to the shoreline. Patty tried to start the boat again but there was a very loud backfire from the motor. On the third try, the boat fired up and Patty pulled away.

When the couple ran out of the door, Kathy had jumped from her seat and headed out the door behind them.

At that same moment, Priscilla had stood up and announced, "I feel ill. I'm going to the bathroom."

The others sat and stared not knowing what to do. Kathy returned, "Where is mom? Since I move so slowly, by the time I got out the door, all I could see was Patty pulling away in her airboat and Richard was nowhere around, so I came back. That poor girl now realizes the truth. I never blamed her for the breakup. In truth, I knew about the others."

"Maybe I should check on Priscilla," said Jean.

Jean was headed to the restroom as Priscilla emerged. "Priscilla, are you alright? You look so pale. Let me help you to the chair."

Priscilla answered, "I think I will take that drink now, if you don't mind. I threw up and felt like I would faint. I was afraid to come out yet in case the bout wasn't over."

After Priscilla finished her drink, it was decided they had better leave. Jean said, "Richard never returned to the bar after the scene."

Belinda said, "Probably he was too embarrassed. I would have been. So much for Richard having a financial partner. I think I will give Patty's grandparents a call when I get home. I don't want to gossip but I really am worried about her."

Chapter 23 – Miriam's Visit

The following day, Jean arrived alone for afternoon tea. "Where is everybody? I'm feeling left out," said Fannie.

Jean said, "You should." She sat down and began the long story of the divorce and the attempt of a celebration that felt more like a disaster before they got home. Fannie and Jean had a relationship that was on a different level from the others. They had partnered on many adventures and had each other's backs in good times and bad. Best friends for over 30 years, they had no secrets from each other. Jean told Fannie about the meeting with Helen at Mr. Craft's office and the statement Vic made about the ReSol's not using another attorney. She shared the good news about Alan helping Jerry to feel better and the great time the boys had with serious gamers at the competition the previous night. Fannie sat quietly and listened, only stopping twice when customers entered the store. She could tell Jean was troubled but didn't understand why.

After the customers left, Fannie sat down again with her friend. "Are you expecting something to happen?"

Jean nodded yes.

"I've got news for you, too," said Fannie. "Yesterday, that skinny woman from the theatre group came in here. She had on a wig and sunglasses. She was dressed in a cheap cotton dress and no makeup. I don't know who she thought she was fooling but it certainly didn't fool me. I knew who she was right away. I pretended I didn't know her. I kept playing with her saying things like, 'Haven't I seen you before?' or 'You seem familiar.' She kept saying she was sure we had never met. She walked through and touched everything in the store when I notice she was wearing gloves. It's not even cold out. She kept trying to get me from behind the counter, pretending to have a sudden headache and needing medicine. Then she tried to say she thought food would help and asked if I could go next door and get something for her to eat. I told her that if she was too ill to walk next door that Gloria would deliver. I also said if she was that ill maybe I should call 911. She was so mad. She spent a lot of time paying attention to the Wyatt Earp outfit. She asked why there weren't any guns in the holsters. I said it was because I hated guns and wouldn't even display toys guns in the store. I told her that if they were out, kids would run through the store pretending to shoot one another. She asked if the outfit was for sale and I told her no because the window display brought customers into the store. I told her to give me her number and I would call if I changed my mind but she refused to do that. She left after that. I really refused because I didn't want to sell it without asking Nick if it was needed for his investigation."

"Why would she come here?" asked Jean. "Do you think Nick is questioning her about the body on the beach?"

Fannie was very serious, "You need to know that Nick is in trouble because his boss thinks he is telling you about his investigations. He could get fired. He is so close to his 20 years and a retirement package, you can't mess this up for him. I promised not to tell you that. I also promised not to tell you about his questioning me but I think it would be the best to tell you everything to keep you out of his case. He was at a dead end regarding the body on the beach when the type of bullet came back as being the same kind used with the gun we found. He called it gut instinct and began checking with the theatre group about the dead body. After all, a real gun in the prop box is just not right. It turns out he was probably right. He didn't tell me that but when I called to tell him about the woman showing up at the store, he was very concerned. He came down and interviewed me again. He wants me to have someone in the store with me. I asked if I was in danger and he said he didn't think so, but I was to use extra precautions from now on. I went to see Gloria and Buddy. They gave me this loud whistle and their number not just to the store but also to their private cell phones. Buddy said he would come immediately if I whistled or called. He is even bringing his gun to work. Here I thought Buddy hated me and yet he is so concerned."

Jean laughed, "Who would he have to embarrass him and give him a hard time if it wasn't for you? Now I'm concerned too. Maybe we can take shifts working the store with you. We can give Priscilla mornings since for some strange reason she gets up so early. I will check with Belinda and Jo so see what works best for their schedules. We can ask Steve to be here during our water times."

Fannie was starting to get annoyed. "I'm not going to have you guys smothering me. I need alone time. I say no to your plan."

Jean was trying to reason with her friend. "This is only until Nick catches the killer. I care about you and you're being selfish."

"Selfish? Me? How do you figure that?" shouted Fannie.

"I love and care about you and if something happened to you then I would feel guilty the rest of my life. You would rather put yourself in danger than let us spend time with you?" Jean reasoned.

Fannie softened her position, "I don't think you would really be all that much protection anyway."

Jean, being playful, said, "I know how to use a gun. Maybe we can get another one and keep it here so I would have a weapon."

Fannie started to react in anger until she saw it was Jean's attempt at humor.

Jean made calls and a schedule was set for that week. "Actually, I will enjoy having Steve hanging around. He is so smart that we can have interesting conversations."

Chapter 24 – Nick and Mrs. Jones

Nick and Janice were hot on the trail of the killer. They were sure they were on the right track with the theatre group, especially since Miriam had shown up at Fannie's store. Now they needed to gather evidence to prove she was guilty of the crime. Janice was in the office going through the boxes they received from the landlord. Nick thought he would get more from the people of Abletown if he was alone. Fannie told him that Belinda and Steve had attended productions at the theatre a few times. As much as Nick wanted to find his leads somewhere else, he decided to call Steve to find out if he had anything that would help. He didn't want this investigation to get back to Jean. Belinda would tell Jean everything so he hoped Steve would keep silent about his inquires if Nick asked him to do so.

"Yes, I know how the girls can be," said Steve. "You wouldn't believe the planning about the party we had, thinking about what the 'undesirables' might do and say. I can see all of them under your feet, so don't worry, I won't say a word. Did you know that Mrs. Jones on Fifth Street and her friend, Mrs. Anderson, usher there on occasion? They might have more information than I do. Miriam acts very nice to Belinda and I when we go. She's not someone we feel close to, but she knows we are members of other theatre groups and is always trying to get us to join."

That interview led to the arrival of the detective at the door of Mrs. Jones' house. "Nick, how good to see you. What can I do for you? Come in and have a seat. Can I get you some coffee?"

Nick accepted the offer. The best ways to have someone give you the information you need is to have them relaxed and enjoying the conversation. "I understand you volunteer at the theatre as an usher. Do you enjoy that?"

Mrs. Jones smiled, "I most certainly do. My late husband and I always enjoyed a good play. We would vacation in New York City just to go to plays on Broadway. I was so lonely after my husband died. I hate going out alone. To be quite frank about it, my income has been greatly reduced, and I will probably never be able to afford Broadway again. By volunteering, I have a purpose for being there. The other ladies and gentlemen that usher sit together in the back to watch the plays. I get to see the productions for free and I'm not alone. In fact, I've made many good friends. A couple of the other ladies and I go out to dinner before we work at the play. We also do other activities together. I found out I'm not alone as far as mature ladies that are widowed and with a limited income. This volunteering has opened up a new world for me. I don't think I will ever be as happy as when my husband was alive but I'm enjoying life again."

Nick patted Mrs. Jones' hand. "You are a lovely person and I'm so glad to know you are able to get out and enjoy life. Do you know Judith Lane that worked at the theatre?"

"Ah, yes. She is such a sweet young girl. She was always so nice to the ushers. She would serve us drinks as we watched the show. If one of us called in sick, she would assure us it was ok. She would often fill in for someone that was out. She was very quiet and loved to listen for hours to our stories. When we talked, she would always be concerned if someone needed help at home. She even talked Art into coming over to help me hang a picture once at no charge. Everyone loves her but we haven't seen her in a long while. Miriam said she left unexpected, something about being needed at home. I do miss her."

Nick loved the way Mrs. Jones would talk, saying everything on her mind without his having to ask questions other than a lead in. "Do you like Miriam Highland?"

Mrs. Jones' expression told more than she knew and the answer had been no. "Miriam is unusual, very bold. She does an excellent job at running the theatre. She really knows her business. The productions are always top-of-the-line. She comes by and thanks the ushers for being there at each performance but she doesn't come across as sincere. I sometimes doubt if she even knows my name. She does when she calls and asks me to work but she has never called me by name when speaking to me face to face. Don't you think that is an indication of not really caring about me as a person?"

Nick nodded his head in agreement. "That seems odd to me. Did you ever notice the interaction between Miriam and Judith?"

A startled expression came over Mrs. Jones' face. "Nick, are you here on a professional basis?"

Nick didn't want to tell Mrs. Jones about Judith until a positive identification was made. "I guess you could say professional but I am enjoying the visit so much, I promise it will be personal next time. I also want to tell you that if you need anyone to help around the house, I would be glad to. I'm not that handy but I could certainly hang a picture for you."

Mrs. Jones smiled with delight. "It is so good to know I can call on you. I don't suppose you can tell me what the professional business is about?"

Nick shook his head no, "As soon as I can, I will tell you the story but right now it wouldn't be best. I hope you trust me on that point."

Mrs. Jones was enjoying Nick's company so much that she was more than willing to continue. "Miriam treated Judith like she treats everyone. Judith was below her. Judith was there to obey her commands. I have never seen anything negative between them but they didn't appear to have a close or personal relationship, strictly boss and employee. Judith didn't seem to mind but accepted her role."

Nick continued his questions, "Do you remember anything special or odd happening when you work there?"

Mrs. Jones thought, "I'm not sure what you are looking for. Let me think. This is really minor and might not be important, but the Creighton family has season tickets. When someone comes in using their tickets, Miriam said to always let her seat them. I'm assuming it is because they are the biggest donors. In fact, they started the production company she works for. They seldom come, but when those tickets come in, we are to get Miriam. One time, a couple I didn't know arrived and handed me two tickets. I started looking for the seats and couldn't find them, so I asked Miriam who got very angry with me. She said she told me to always let her sit the customers with the Creighton tickets. I told her I didn't know these people had anything to do with the Creighton family or I would have. Miriam then acted nicer and said she understood I didn't know, but if the seats 140 to 146 ever came in again, to come and get her. I promised I would. Is that important? I hope I'm not boring you with my babbling."

Nick used his most sincere voice when he said, "Not at all. You have been most helpful. I have truly enjoyed this visit but had better get back to work. Mrs. Jones, I'm not trying to be melodramatic, but can you please not say anything about our conversation to anyone, especially anyone to do with the theatre? Not that the theatre has done anything wrong but you know how negative rumors can spread. I wouldn't want the theatre to get a bad name because people think the police are looking into them."

Mrs. Jones was already trying to think of a task for Nick to do so he would visit again as she waved goodbye from the porch and wished Nick good luck at work. Jean would be sure to hear about the visit due to small town gossip. He worried Mrs. Jones would speak to people about the conversation in spite of his request.

Chapter 25 – Another Crime Scene

Nick was headed back to the office to get Janice. He was planning a visit to the Creighton household when he received a call from her. "Nick, there has been a body found and we are to investigate. You aren't that far away so I will drive over and meet you there." He was the first on the scene at the bar on the pier.

"Down here," motioned the owner of the pub. A walking path behind the bar led through a wooded area to the water's edge that ended close to the pier. Half in and half out of the water was the body of a man lying face down. He had been shot though the stomach. "He might not have died immediately." The owner continued. "I'm a hunter myself. I bet he suffered before he died. I smelled something rotten when I was cleaning up. That's when I found him. I didn't touch him, just walked over to check and knew he was a goner."

The remaining police units had arrived. Janice was hurrying to join him, and the remainder of the crew started their jobs of getting photographs, gathering evidence, and waiting instructions from the officers in charge. Nick turned to Janice, "You better take charge and call the office. Let them know I'm acquainted with the victim. His name is Richard ReSol."

Janice may have been the junior officer at one time but not now. She was every bit his equal. He sat on the porch of the pub drinking an iced tea and let her work. He was glad they were partners and had been for years. He had total respect for her ability and trusted her to have his back in any situation. Two other detectives arrived to take over the case. He would have to excuse himself because he knew the victim and his family. Janice joined him after she got the other two detectives updated on the case.

"What is going on? How close were you to Mr. ReSol?" She was very serious, not just because of the job but because of her concern that he and Richard had been friends. The other two detectives joined after completing their work with the body and crime scene.

He knew the questioning would begin and he also knew he had to tell the truth, even if Jean would be livid with him. "I only saw Richard twice, once at a ballroom dance and once at a pool party at Jean's." The others showed their surprise but kept silent and let him

154

talk. Nick told the full story of seeing Richard out with his girlfriend, then how later that night Richard left his wife and boys. He told the full story of the pool party. He totally didn't want to answer the final question, if he knew anyone that wanted to kill Richard or made threats against him. He tried to soften the words he heard Priscilla say the morning after Richard left. He told them he knew Priscilla and those words were just a mother and grandmother speaking in shock. He said Priscilla was too kind and could never hurt anyone but he knew he had already caused a lot of harm. Even being one of the police, he had to endure long hours of questions. All the while he worried how Jean would react.

Chapter 26 – Initial Questioning

Detectives Ruiz and Jonas arrived at the Home at the same time as Nick and Janice. "You know you are out of the investigation. We would appreciate it if you would leave and let us handle it."

Nick was friends with the other detectives so he didn't take their comments personally. "You know Jean. She will handle this better with Janice and me here for support. We don't plan to interfere and will leave as soon as we feel Jean and Priscilla are over the shock and ready for the interviews."

Jean was not at home. She was at Fannie's store guarding her friend. The detectives knocked on the door of Priscilla's room but she wasn't home either. Priscilla had spent the night at her daughter's house to be supportive of her and her grandsons. Nick called and asked Jean to return to her apartment. "Who is going to babysit Fannie?" she asked, which earned her a dirty look from her friend.

Fannie assured her friend that with Gloria and Buddy next door and the busy crowd in the store that day that she would be fine. Jean dropped in to let Buddy know she was leaving and that Fannie would be alone. She tried to call Steve as she walked home. He said he would be free in about a half hour and would take her shift at the store.

Jean was stunned and leery as she entered her room. It was unusual but not a surprise to see Nick and Janice but the other two detectives took the lead in the conversation. She saw them at some functions with Nick and had been introduced but really didn't know them well. Upon their suggestion, she sat down. "Richard ReSol is dead. We found him this morning. We came to talk to Priscilla, but since she isn't here, we decided to talk with you first so we won't have to come back."

Jean shot a look at Nick who just nodded. She knew he had told what he had heard. She knew she now had to disclose the whole truth as well. She was angry that her friend was under suspicion and Nick knew it.

The next hour was questioning about her friend, Kathy and Richard. Jean answered each one honestly and completely but never offered additional information. When the detectives brought up the comment about what Priscilla had said, 'I hate him. I wish he was dead,' Jean started scolding them.

"That's right. That's exactly what she said. She didn't say I am going to kill him. She didn't threaten him. She just realized her daughter and grandsons would be better off without him in their lives. Realizing the world would be a better place without someone in it doesn't mean you are going to do anything about it. I don't think there is a single person that wouldn't like someone to be gone, but that doesn't mean they would ever commit murder. Priscilla is the most kind and gentle person I know and so is Kathy. In spite of his actions, they have gone overboard to be nice to him and even to Patty."

When questioned about the activities the night before, Jean had to fight back the tears. If she told the truth, she knew it would look bad for her friend. There were too many people that saw them at the pub to lie or omit complete answers. Everyone at the table knew Priscilla had gone to the bathroom for a very long time. Everyone knows there are two doors to the bathroom, one that entered the pub and one that exited outside for the outdoor diners to use. Everyone knew Richard left the bar at the same time Priscilla was missing from the table and never returned. She felt like Judas as she answered the questions. She felt she was driving the nails in the hands of her friend as she told the truth.

Nick was waiting outside her door and entered as Ruiz and Jonas left. Jean didn't hide her anger, "Why aren't you going to Priscilla and Kathy? Are those goons going to march in and attack them? What will those poor boys think?"

Nick said, "You are overreacting. The boys are in school and they will let Kathy handle telling them."

Jean continued her planning, "We need to go up there. We need to be there for them."

Nick sighed, "You know Ruiz and Jonas. They are doing their job and are not heartless monsters." Nick pulled out his phone. He called Ruiz and asked if Jean could come up and be with the boys when they returned from school. They actually welcomed the idea so they could take Kathy and Priscilla to the station for questioning. Jean jumped in her car immediately and began her journey.

When Jean arrived, the detectives had already told Priscilla and Kathy that Richard was dead. Kathy was crying when she said, "The boys will be devastated." When the detective told Kathy that she and Priscilla had to go downtown for questioning Kathy begged, "Can we do the questioning here? I need to let them know. I can't just leave them." The detectives really did have a heart, and agreed to question Kathy before they got home but wanted to take Priscilla downtown before they arrived.

Jean hugged the boys when then arrived. One look at their mother and the strange men told them something was really wrong. Jerry began to shout, "What's wrong? What is going on?" Kathy held them close as she told them that their father had died. She didn't say he was murdered and no one corrected that omission. The boys cried and held tight to their mother as the detectives motioned for Jean to walk them to their car.

Ruiz turned to Jean, "I know this is hard. We are glad you are there for them."

Jean softened her anger with this show of kindness, "You are wrong if you think it was Priscilla. I know it looks bad but I know her and know she would never kill anyone."

Jonas said, "Jean, we are not after anyone but we have to follow where the clues lead."

Chapter 27 – Aftershock

The boys were unable to eat, went to bed, and cried themselves to sleep. Jean was sitting with Jerry, and Kathy sat beside Craig. Kathy did her share of crying, too. They were in the kitchen when Priscilla walked in. Jean made hot toddies for all three of them. That was usually her medicine for colds but figured it was good for this crisis, too.

"They think I did it," Priscilla said without a lot of emotion. "I didn't. I hated what he did to Kathy and the boys, but I would never take their father from them."

Jean hugged her, "I know you. You would never hurt anyone."

The entire evening continued between the sorrow and the shock. Only time, a long time, would make things look brighter.

Priscilla and Kathy went to sleep next to the boys in case they awoke in the night. Jean made a bed on the couch. Not yet asleep, Jean got a call from Fannie. She forgot to make sure protection patrol was continuing but the group of friends had that under control. They didn't really need Jean to lead them, or boss them as some might say.

"What is going on? When you didn't come back, I got worried. Steve said Nick, Janice and two other men were at the Home. He said you took off in the car like you were crazy. I'm in my apartment now and see Richard is dead. It's on the news."

Jean caught her friend up on the events in general. She didn't go into detail about the case against Priscilla and how guilty she felt telling to the police about Priscilla being away from the table at the time of the murder. She held to the false hope that nothing would become of it. She prayed the killer would be found and the police would leave her friend alone.

The next morning, Kathy called Helen to see if she was taking care of the arrangements for the funeral. It would be a few days because the body was being held with the medical examiner until they felt they had everything they needed.

Helen was her usual rude self, "You are not his wife. You are not a part of the family. I wouldn't even tell you when and where if it wasn't for the boys. Tell your mother she will not be welcomed at the service.

My son was murdered and I wouldn't be surprised if you two did it."

Kathy was trying hard not to explode. "You're his stepmother and you were never that close to Richard. This isn't about us, it is about the boys. I will make sure my sons are protected from you when we are saying goodbye to their father." She slammed down the phone. "She is the picture of true evil."

Jean went outside and called Nick. He had called the night before to make sure everyone was ok and to offer to be there. Jean appreciated the offer but thought best not to have the police, even Nick, around Priscilla. She was calling to see if she could get any updates.

"I know you can't say much on an open investigation, but do they really believe it was Priscilla? Are they coming for her? I don't want the boys to see that happen. I know you can't say much but please warn me if something is about to hit."

Nick confirmed that he couldn't say anything and also that he would be out of the loop due to personal involvement. "It will be alright. I believe the truth prevails." He asked to meet for dinner that night and Jean accepted the date.

Chapter 28 – The Creighton Family

Nick and Janice had their own case to conclude. They left to visit the Creighton household. The rich were usually not cooperative. They arrived at the front door only to be told neither Mr. nor Mrs. Creighton were home. The eldest son, Donald, agreed to meet with them in the study.

"I would say welcome but I can't imagine that the police at the front door are bringing good news. My parents are out and I wondered if I could be of help, or do you need to talk to them only?"

Nick tried to act friendly and not act like a hard-nosed detective who is out to get information from someone. "We would very much appreciate your time. Are you involved with the theatre in which your father is the head of the board of directors?"

Donald gave a laugh that was more of a snort, "No, that's my father's project. Can you tell me what this is about?"

Nick obliged, "Judith Lane worked at the theatre a few months ago, and her body was found washed up on the beach."

Donald gave a curious look, "Wasn't that a while back?"

Janice didn't want to appear uninvolved so she answered, "There was no identification on the body. There was no missing person report. It has taken a while for us to find out her identity, but we are out to do her justice now. Did you know her or anything about her?"

Donald continued to be cooperative. "I can't say I knew her or ever spoke to her except to exchange pleasantries. She seemed nice and when I did go to a show, she was very professional at her job. She struck me as intelligent for some reason. She seemed smart with people. I notice that when customers and volunteers had questions, they would go to her instead of Miriam. By being here, are you insinuating that her death had something to do with the theatre?"

Nick answered, "No. It is standard procedure to investigate all possible leads, which includes the person's place of employment. Do you have any information that might help us? Do you think we might speak to your mother and father about this?"

Donald then showed more emotion, "I don't know more than I told you. I don't want you talking to my mother about this! Dad should be able to help you. When I said this is my father's project that means the rest of the family has nothing to do with it. Miriam is my father's mistress. The family knows about her but pretends not to for the sake of appearance. Dad lets Miriam live on his yacht called "My Dreams". He is probably there now. Mom hates boats so it is safe she won't go there. Every now and then, Mom makes Dad take her to a play just to let Miriam know she isn't about to replace her. I show up with my wife once in a while but can't stand to go to the theatre because I hate Miriam. My wife doesn't know about the affair to my knowledge, so she doesn't understand my reluctance to be there. The theatre is Miriam's toy and her source of income. She feels big and important in the community. My dad and his friends use it as a tax write-off. Miriam knows her place. She will never be high society and Dad would never leave my mother for her. She tows the line and does what she is permitted because if she makes a mistake, Dad will dump her. There is always another woman willing to be his mistress so she isn't secure in her relationship. My dad always keeps a toy for his use. I don't care how rich you are or what the status is with your current wife, but it is just wrong."

The detectives got directions to the yacht and thanked Donald for his honesty.

In the car, Janice said, "Wow! Didn't see that coming out of the interview, did you?"

Nick laughed, "No. It's nice to know that Donald is a good person and not following the example his father has provided."

The yacht was easy to find. The detectives just looked for the biggest and the best.

"Ahoy, permission to come aboard," called Nick.

"That's not just an old movie thing?" asked Janice.

Mr. Creighton came to the rail smiling and waved them to come on.

Nick repeated the story of what happened to Judith and assured him that the theatre wasn't under investigation.

Mr. Creighton, while remaining formal, did seem jovial and willing to be interviewed. "I remember Judith, very nice, professional and quiet. I would speak to her when I was there but never about personal matters. I was disappointed when she left. I even pushed for her to go full- time. Since you say my son told you of my involvement with Miriam, there is no point in denying it. I hoped Judith would work out and take on more responsibilities so that Miriam and I could travel more. Miriam likes to keep a tight hold on the theatre so she didn't like the idea of sharing the work load."

A few more questions didn't manifest into any real clues. Mr. Creighton walked the detectives around the yacht. Nick stopped, "Isn't that a skeet shoot?"

"Yes, it is. Do you shoot?"

Nick replied, "Yes, for fun but I don't follow the sport. Do you participate in competitions? Isn't it odd to be on a boat?"

Mr. Creighton laughed, "I do have a love of guns. There is a whole collection in the next room from where we were talking. I don't compete but Miriam does. She is very good. She gets very little time to travel to tournaments now but she does local events. Shooting skeet from your ship is quite the rage. They even have them on cruise ships. A lot of boat owners have one because there are so many laws about when and where you can fire a gun. It is easier to go out into international water to practice your shooting."

Janice looked alive with excitement. "Do you own any .45 Colts with ivory-carved handles?"

Mr. Creighton didn't realize it was part of the investigation, "Yes, I do. Are you a gun enthusiast, also? Would you like to see them?"

Janice smile, "Oh yes, very much so."

They went below and Mr. Creighton headed to a drawer, but when he opened it, he had a surprised look on his face. "My .45 that was owned by my great grandfather is missing!"

Nick and Janice immediately offered to file the report. After completing the questions, Mr. Creighton looked very stern. "Why did you ask about that exact type of gun? You even asked about the handles."

Nick answered, "There was one found in an antique store and the proprietor called me."

Mr. Creighton looked relieved, "Then I might get it back. How did it get there?"

Nick didn't want to tell Mr. Creighton too much for fear of him tipping off Miriam Highland. "Unfortunately, the gun was stolen out of the store before I could get there. We are on the trail looking for it now. I'm not positive how it got to the store but will follow up with an interview with the owner. Now that we think it might be yours, I will give it a higher priority."

Mr. Creighton thanked them sincerely. His eagerness for the return of the gun was apparent.

Chapter 29 – The Gun Returns

"It was horrible," Jean was telling Fannie as she sat having a cup of tea to calm her nerves. "Helen made it clear that Priscilla wasn't to attend the funeral. We didn't want Kathy and the boys to go alone, so Nick and I went with them. Charles is in really bad shape. He kept shaking his head and crying. He said he couldn't believe it over and over again. Vic, Charles ReSol's attorney, was there and very supportive of his client. It appears Richard had no friends. There was a small crowd but they were all there for Charles. He accepted the hugs and support of his friends but was unable to enter into conversation. He had to be led around and even told what to do. It has been a little time since the murder but it was like he was in shock."

Fannie said, "I'm sure he has some form of dementia. It isn't unusual for something as serious as the loss of a son to push someone with diminished capacity over the edge. I almost wish I had gone because I would know how to deal with someone in his condition."

Jean continued, "No one is admitting he has a condition. I heard Barb asking Helen about Charles being so despondent, and she said it was the fact that it was his only child. Alex and Barb showed up but Patty was noticeably absent. The boys were happy to see Alex and Barb. They were the only ones to show kindness to Kathy and the boys. Most people acted like they weren't even there, especially Helen. I really dislike that woman."

Fannie was animated when she said, "Speaking of that woman, Helen was in the store the other day."

Jean was surprised. "What? She came here after her snobbish comments to you at the pool party? She didn't hide the fact she didn't like you. What did she want?"

"Can you believe she had clothes she wanted to sell on consignment? I was in the back of the store showing some furniture to a couple and they took a long time to decide if they wanted the leather sofa and chair. I had to use a little patience with them but ended up not only selling the furniture but talked them into getting tables, lamps, and a picture. When I came to the front, she was standing on the side of the counter. She was moving so she might have been behind the counter. I tried not to be conspicuous but I did check the money box to make sure nothing was missing."

Jean laughed, "With all their money, I doubt she would be after yours."

Fannie was offended, "For being such a great detective, you aren't thinking of all the possibilities. Maybe she is mentally sick and stealing gives her a thrill. Maybe she wants to hurt me by taking my profits. The fact that she acted like an old friend tells me she was up to no good. She talked about how nice my store was and she felt she would get the best profit for her items if they were sold here. You're right, she doesn't need money so why not just give the clothes to charity as a tax write-off?"

"You are a genius! Those are very good questions. What was she up to? Who was on Fannie watch at the time? Maybe they saw something." Jean felt stupid she hadn't seen the possibilities for herself.

Fannie looked at her friend, "You were supposed to be. It was the day they found Richard's body. Nick called for you to go to your apartment. Steve hadn't arrived yet so no one was at the front of the store. I heard someone come in and I shouted I would be right there. I looked to the front, and at first I didn't see anyone so I went back to the customers. When we came up to pay for the purchase and schedule delivery, she was standing there. She had to be in the store 5 or 10 minutes before I knew it."

Jean's mind wasn't working slowly any longer. She ran to the back room and grabbed the key from the hook, then raced to the drawer. The gun was lying on top of the other items inside. "Now to prove it," she said.

Fannie's mouth was hanging open, "You don't know it was Helen. Everyone has worked at the store since the murder, including Priscilla. They might say she put it in there when I went to the bakery. What do we do?"

"There's only one thing to do. We can't hide evidence and I know Nick needs this gun to prove who killed Judith Lane. I know Richard was shot but I don't know the caliber. We don't have a choice," said Jean as she called Nick.

Chapter 30 – Jean's Call

Nick didn't take the call because he and Janice were in the boss's office. Janice's phone began to ring. She noticed it was Jean and shot a glance to Nick. "What is going on?" growled the head detective.

"Nothing that can't wait until we are through here," replied Janice.

As soon as they could escape, Nick called Jean, "I don't appreciate you calling Janice when I didn't pick up. We were in a meeting and couldn't be disturbed."

"THE GUN!" Jean stated before realizing how loudly she exclaimed. She then lowered her voice, "The gun is back!"

Nick was shocked, "What? When?"

"I'm at Fannie's. It was in the locked drawer. I don't believe anyone has looked in there since it went missing," explained Jean.

Nick's boss was standing behind him, "How did that woman get involved in another case?"

So Nick could continue getting information from Jean, Janice told the boss, "She doesn't know it was related to a case. Her friend Fannie found a gun in a box she got at an auction. They were saving it for Nick to see but it was stolen from the store before he arrived. I guess now it is back. She is just letting us know. She's just excited because who would return a stolen gun? I assure you she knows nothing about our case."

Not totally believing the story, he shouted, "Well, get that gun before it goes missing again!"

When Janice and Nick walked into the store, the first words out of Jean's mouth were, "I bet it was the gun that killed Judith Lane."

Janice whispered to Nick, "I'm so glad the boss didn't hear that statement." Speaking louder to Jean, she asked, "Why would you say that?"

"Elementary, my dear Janice," said Jean. "The gun arrives in the store through a purchase at the auction, dead body washes up killed with a gunshot, then the evil lady from theatre shows up at the store. So it has to be the gun, right?" Nick stood back to let his partner handle Jean.

Janice playfully asked, "Ok Sherlock, why did the gun reappear at the store and who put it there?"

Jean was thinking hard, "I don't know yet but just wait, I will figure it out."

Nick gave Jean a kiss on the cheek, "Will you please call us limited intelligent detectives and give us a clue when you do?"

Jean pouted, "You should be thanking me and also thanking Fannie. Instead, you act like we are stupid."

Nick laughed, "Both of you are anything but stupid. I'm sure you will figure it out."

Jean stated, "Helen put the gun in the drawer. I didn't want to tell you because you think I have it out for the lady, but I know it was Helen."

Nick was serious, "Why do you say that? Did anyone see Helen with the gun? Did anyone see Helen put it in the drawer? What evidence or proof do you have? Are you going to risk being sued for slander? Jean, you have to watch what you say. Fannie, I need a list of everyone you can think of that either worked at the store or was in here."

Fannie was irritated because of how Nick just acted. "That's impossible. Most of the people that enter the store, I don't even know their names. How far back do you want this list to go?"

As Fannie and Nick talked in a less-than-friendly way, Janice took Jean aside, "Jean, he's right. You could get in trouble so be careful of what you say and to whom. He really is just trying to let you know how serious something you say can be. Only Fannie, Nick, and I heard you so that's ok. We won't tell anyone. Just be careful, ok?"

Jean was angry, "No, it isn't ok. He will rat me out just like he did with Priscilla when she said, 'I hate him and wish he was dead'."

Janice tried to hug Jean but Jean pushed her aside and hurried out the door.

Chapter 31 – The Arrest

"You have a problem with Jean right now. I know you didn't do anything wrong but she isn't seeing it that way," warned Janice when she was alone with Nick.

Nick tried to justify his actions, "You're right, I didn't do anything wrong. Did she think I would lie and sabotage my job or the investigation?"

Janice knew when to keep her mouth shut. After so many happy years together, she hated to see the friction between the usually loving, happy couple.

Ballistic tests proved the gun was used to murder Judith Lane. The tests also proved the same gun was used for the Richard ReSol murder.

The fingerprints on the handle of the gun and the trigger area were wiped clean, but there were fingerprints on the top of the gun and the cylinder that belonged to Priscilla. Two bullets had been fired with four rounds still available.

Ruiz and Jonas were satisfied with the case they had built against Priscilla. They had the motive of Richard leaving his wife and kids. They had Priscilla's opportunity with, not only access to the gun, but being at the pub at the time of the murder. They even had an officer of the law hear her wishing for his death. They felt this was a very open-and-shut case done by a non-professional criminal who couldn't cover her tracks.

They were in the front car that pulled to the curb, and Nick and Janice were in a second car. The friends, Priscilla, Jo, Jean, Belinda and Eve were on the front porch talking when Jean saw the cars park. She jumped to her feet and was standing at the top of the steps with her hands on her hips. The other ladies formed a circle around Priscilla.

Ruiz and Jonas walked to the top of the steps but Jean wasn't moving. "YOU ARE NOT TAKING MY FRIEND! YOU ARE WRONG! TRY DOING YOUR JOB AND FIND THE REAL KILLER!"

Nick passed the other detectives and put his arms around Jean and whispered, "Come with me and we will talk about this." Jean tried to push him away. He again put his arms around Jean, "You can't help her if you get arrested too. She needs you more on the outside fighting for her than she does sitting in the jail next to her."

Jean had tears running down her face as did all the ladies. "You know she didn't do this. You know Priscilla could never hurt anyone."

Nick kissed Jean and whispered, "You're right. I can't stop them but I'm willing to help you, so please stay calm."

Priscilla was cuffed and taken to the car. Janice was walking with her trying to say comforting words.

Jean ordered Nick, "Go with her and keep her safe."

"Are you going to be ok? Do you want me to stay with you instead?" he asked. Jean shook her head no.

The friends held each other tight while they watched Priscilla being driven away.

Janice rode in the back of the car with Priscilla. Nick took Jean aside and they talked quietly for a few minutes in very quiet voices so no one could hear what was being said.

As soon as Nick's car was out of sight, Jean ordered, "To Fannie's now! We are at war and going to plan our attack!"

Chapter 32 – Attack Plan

The ladies marched into Fannie's store with looks of anger and determination on their faces.

Jean apologized, "I know I'm going to be bossy and I'm sorry, but everyone needs to help for us to get Priscilla free. I'm well aware that things look bad for Priscilla and if I didn't know her so well I could understand the detective's logic, but I do know her and know she didn't do it. We need to start at the beginning. I told everyone not to say anything about the gun to anyone else. Did any of you say anything?"

Eve, Fannie, and Belinda shook their heads no. Josephine looked guilty, "I only told Michael and I know he didn't say anything to anyone."

"Please call and confirm he didn't. This is very serious. Someone told because I'm working on the assumption that nobody in our group of six stole the gun so someone else had to know it was here," said Jean.

Josephine just hung up from talking to Michael, "What are you talking about? I didn't even know the gun was stolen. By the way, Michael didn't tell anyone. He figured it was a fake and we weren't bright enough to know the difference. He wouldn't have said anything anyway. Get back to the stolen gun."

Fannie told the date and details of the break-in. "Only Nick, Jean, and I knew it was stolen and I didn't tell anyone. I was afraid it would be used for a crime. Why else would you steal a gun?"

Jean continued, "I didn't tell anyone about the missing gun and neither did Nick. We know the person that killed Richard stole it and returned it."

Jo asked, "Why return the gun? Why not dump it by the body or in the water?"

Jean didn't hesitate when she said, "To frame someone. Somehow, the person knew Priscilla's prints were on the gun. They wanted the gun to be found. If you used the gun and wiped the prints off, wouldn't you clean the whole gun? The prints were off the handle and trigger but not off the top. It wouldn't be the murderer of Judith Lane because that director was here looking for the gun before Richard's murder but after the gun was stolen."

Eve asked, "Do you know who it is?"

Jean nodded, "Yes, but Nick and Janice keep telling me not to tell. They are worried I might be wrong and be sued for saying something, so let's follow the clues."

Fannie asked, "How do you know about the fingerprints on the gun?"

Josephine answered, "Nick took Jean aside and talked to her before we came."

Fannie warned, "Let's never say that line again. If Nick did tell Jean something like that, he could be fired."

Jean added to the conversation, "Nick didn't exactly tell me. I agree with Fannie to never repeat what we say here to anyone. Let's just find the clues and give them to the police without them knowing our efforts."

Belinda had pulled out index cards and was writing names. "We have Priscilla that we know would never do it. Kathy was at the crime scene and away from the table when the murder occurred."

Jo said, "That would be even worse for Priscilla to find out it was her daughter. She would be livid at us putting her on the suspect list."

Belinda continued, "Patty is definitely a suspect because she was the one with him at the time. They were outside alone before Priscilla and Kathy went outside. We all heard how angry she was. You don't slap someone in public without being angry enough to kill. That would devastate Alex and Barb."

Eve added to the thought, "Do you think either Alex or Barb would kill to protect Patty? We didn't see them but the way we sat with the bar blocking our view, anyone could have been there or outside without us knowing it. Maybe they heard the same proof that Richard was a gold-digger and didn't realize Patty had come to her senses."

Belinda wrote the names down. "Good thought."

Josephine then added her thought, "Helen should be down. She always hated Richard even if she tried to hide it. Charles loved his son so he would never do it, but she is a different story."

Jean continued, "Ok, let's divide up and follow the leads and report back here when we're done. Fannie, you said Helen dropped off things on consignment. Did any of them sell?"

Fannie shook her head no. "There is a coat I like. She hated it. Charles gave it to her because it reminded him of one his mother used to wear. I will buy it myself and move a couple of other things to the back room out of view in case she stops in again."

Jean turned to Eve, "I want you and Fannie to take the money to Helen. Let Fannie do most of the talking and you observe. Go into the bathroom and look around. Try to look anywhere you think is important while Fannie keeps her talking. Be very careful when dealing with Helen. I don't trust her."

"What am I looking for?" asked Eve.

Fannie replied, "We don't know for sure. It could be anything from dirty boots that got mud on them from the water where Richard was killed to a prescription for Charles' dementia. You have to let your eyes observe then figure out what is important. I'll try to find out where they were when Richard was murdered as well as about Charles' condition. I know how to follow a lead, too."

Belinda suggested, "Shouldn't Steve go instead in case there is violence?"

Fannie shook her head no, "Too many people and I know how to handle myself. Eve is more observant than Steve. It would be a great help if he watched the store. He's actually very good at this business and customers love him."

Belinda was calling Steve. "He loves watching the store and will be over soon. I'm not telling him what we're doing. That would be a bad idea."

"Josephine, I'm calling Alan to meet you at Kathy's house. I want you and Kathy to hire Mr. Thomas to defend Priscilla. He is the best criminal lawyer I know. It will probably be tomorrow before bail can be set. Get him over there now to make sure Priscilla understands not to say a word without him in the room. You go with Kathy to try to get Priscilla free, post bail if needed. Find out if she told anyone about the gun. Have Alan stay with the boys. They love him. He needs to find out anything that he can about conversations with Patty, her parents, and Helen that could add light to the investigation. Here is my credit card. I will call and tell them I approve any charges you make. Let me know if you need more."

Josephine flipped the card back to her sister stating, "Priscilla is my friend, too. If it gets too high, we can split the cost but right now I don't want your money. I'm glad this is my assignment. She needs me."

Belinda looked at Jean to see what was next. "Belinda, you and I are calling on Barb and hopefully Patty. I need your connections to get the rich and famous to give me the time of day. We will be good at working information from them together. Fannie, when you get back, try to downplay what is happening. All of us really need to listen to town gossip and dispel anything bad we can about Priscilla. Ok, time for our attack."

Chapter 33 – Evidence Surfaces

Nick was worried about Jean. She could get herself in trouble with her snooping. He knew nothing he could do or say that would stop her. He called Alan hoping he would be his spy, his inside man. Alan told him not to worry, that the investigation was in full swing and they had high hopes of clearing Priscilla. This wasn't the news he wanted. Alan did promise to let Nick know if his mother was headed for trouble.

Nick and Janice had their own murder to finish up. Sometimes it wasn't the question of who did the crime but how to catch them. You can't get too focused on one person just in case you are wrong. He began the process of talking it out with Janice. "We know Miriam told a lie about Judith going to her parents. Is there any hint that maybe she didn't really listen or care why Judith left and just said what came to her head? Access to the gun was limited to the Creighton family and

Miriam. Donald could be wrong about his mother never going to the yacht."

Janice suggested, "We could go by the house to see if she is home. We have the good excuse that we thought her husband might be there. Donald would never let us get to her if he's home."

When they pulled up in the driveway, they saw an elegant-looking woman getting into the back of the Mercedes. When the detectives approached and introduced themselves, she instructed her chauffer to step out of hearing range.

"I heard about your visit. Donald is very protective of me but I'm not the fragile person he believes me to be. I know about the young girl from the theatre and I'm so sorry to hear of her death. I want you to know that I never really talked to her and didn't know her. I'm sorry I can't contribute anything to get her justice. I stay away from the theatre because of Miriam. I have full knowledge of her affair with my husband. She thinks she is special, but in truth, I believe my husband is starting to tire of her and will move on to his next conquest soon. You have to understand that rich men think they have the right to do as they wish. I don't agree with that but I do believe in keeping up the right appearance. My husband has all the money. I could get divorced and walk away with half, but where would that get me? I was hurt the first time I found out about his activities, but after 50 years of marriage, you just accept what you have to. We lead separate lives except for social and family functions and I'm really at peace with that. Do you have any questions?"

The detectives said no and returned to their car. "Wow! Wasn't that the easiest interview we ever did? It's safe to say that this isn't a crime of passion or to keep Judith quiet so the wife wouldn't find out about the affair. What was the motive for Judith's murder?" asked Janice.

Nick said, "If you take away the crime of passion, then usually the answer is to follow the money. We will get a court order and have our guys go over the books. Looking for theft is the only thing I can figure."

They arrived at the boat to find Mr. Creighton waiting for them. He surprised them with, "My wife called and said you came by the house looking for me. Since you knew I would probably be here, I take it you wanted to interview her. Isn't she the most spectacular woman in the world?"

Janice overstepped good judgment when she answered, "Yes, she is. It's nice to know you can appreciate her great qualities."

Nick was trying to move the conversation away from personal opinions quickly. "I have good news for you, sir. We have found your gun."

The delight showed on Mr. Creighton's face, "Great! Where is it?"

"Well, I guess this is a good news, bad news type of visit. We have your gun and it will be returned to you, but it was used in two homicides. It is currently being held for evidence. I wanted you to know it was found and that you will get the gun back, eventually."

Mr. Creighton's good humor was returning, "You are right. I'm so pleased to hear it. You said two homicides, can I ask whom?"

Janice, trying to get back in good graces, said, "Since both murders are public knowledge, I don't suppose it would hurt to tell you. Judith Lane was the first victim and Richard ReSol was the second."

Mr. Creighton was thinking, "I'm so sorry to hear about both, really. I don't ever remember meeting a ReSol, but my big concern is Judith. This isn't looking good. I have something to show you." They went to his computer on the deck below. "I got this email a long time ago. I didn't recognize the party sending the email. Memorylane was the title that sent it. I figured it was an advertisement so I just deleted it. I was expecting an email from a friend and when it didn't come through, I had my computer guy come out to see what happened to it. He found that there were instructions that anything from Memorylane was to be quarantined. I didn't even know I had a quarantine box. We searched though the computer and I printed out any emails and responses. I was greatly disturbed and was trying to decide if I should call you or ask Miriam about them. This one said they have important information for me and asked if we could meet. This one was from my computer, which I didn't send, inviting them to the yacht on Saturday evening. I looked on my calendar and my wife and I were attending a fundraiser on that evening for the governor so we were at the capital all weekend. What do you think I should do?"

Nick knew the evidence of when and where was just handed to him. "First, don't say anything to Miriam. There is a risk she might see through you. Can you make an excuse to leave town for a few days? Will you permit us to have a crime lab go over the boat?"

Sorrow showed on Mr. Creighton's face. "Miriam lives here. I can easily have a reason for my wife and I to leave town. I usually don't tell Miriam where I'm going or what I'm doing. It is best not to disclose your real life to your mistress so my absence will not be questioned. How to get her off the yacht is another matter."

Nick and Janice conferred a few minutes. It was decided that any real evidence that may have been on the yacht would have been destroyed by now or would still be there later. They didn't want to finish playing their hand too soon, so they decided to take what evidence they had to see if they could get a warrant for Miriam's arrest.

Chapter 34 – Visiting Barb and Patty

Belinda and Jean arrived at her parent's house and called Barb. "Hi," said Belinda, "We are in town and wanted to stop by for a visit, if that would be alright with you."

Barb was more than happy to extend an invitation to lunch, "Patty has been so depressed that she won't leave the house. She seldom comes out of her room. She mentioned once before that she enjoyed talking to you, Belinda. She feels you understand her."

Belinda, in her usually cheerful voice, said, "Sure, I would be glad to talk with her. Maybe you can make an excuse to leave with Jean so we can be alone after lunch."

Patty greeted them as soon as they came in the door. "I'm so happy to see you, Belinda." She leaned in and whispered, "Do you think we can get time alone?"

Belinda smiled, "I bet that can be arranged."

Lunch was light but filling. Barb said, "Jean, this is your first visit to our home. Would you like me to show you around? As a writer, I bet you will enjoy seeing our library." Jean gladly accepted. "Would you like to join us, Belinda?"

Belinda, knowing this was a cover to keep Patty from seeing the set-up, declined. "Patty, it is such a lovely day. Do you think we could have our coffee on the patio?"

"Oh, that would be wonderful. Thank you for the suggestion." As soon as they were out of earshot, Patty couldn't wait to spill her heart out. "I was at a shower for a friend of mine. My friends knew I was dating a mystery man but they didn't know who. They teased me asking when they would meet this great lover that finally won my heart. They also knew I was taking dancing lessons and asked about my progress. One friend after another talked about this dance instructor that had made passes at them, and they knew he was only after their money. The two that dated him said they had to pay for everything because he had no money. They talked about what a horrible person he was and how he mistreated his wife. Suddenly, one of them said his name, Richard ReSol. I first thought my grandparents had put them up to telling the story, but they had pictures of him on their cell phones. It's not like it was a picture of just him. It was pictures of him at a party with his arm around different girls. I knew then that my grandparents were right all along. I was thankful my friends didn't know I was dating Richard. I laughed at their stories and promised they would meet my guy soon enough. I couldn't wait to get out of there. I told my grandparents that I had a change of heart about Richard and wanted to move home. I didn't tell them why. I just said that he wasn't for me. I thought about it and realized that I did pay for everything. I thought about Kathy and felt bad. She was so nice to me even when I was a snob. I went to the bar in my grandfather's airboat that night. If I was in a car, I was afraid he would follow me after I broke the engagement. I slapped him and ended it. He followed me to the airboat and was trying to grab me. He tried to explain his past but I knew no matter what he said, it was a lie. I hit him with an oar we keep in the boat in case the motor broke. He fell back into the water and was swimming to the shore. I wanted to get out of there so badly. The boat wouldn't start but I kept trying. The boat made a loud backfire, but then finally came to life. I raced out of there. I never saw him after the fall from the dock. I feel so horrible. While I hate him, I feel like his death was my fault." Patty kept wiping away the tears in case her grandmother returned. She didn't want to be seen crying.

Belinda was trying to calm Patty down. "You sure had a lot of worry built up inside you. I'm glad to be here for you to unload those feelings. It isn't your fault. If Richard is dead, it was probably his fault. He wasn't very nice and made enemies by his choices. I'm so glad you found out before you married him."

Patty asked, "Belinda, you're my friend. If you knew he was so bad, why didn't you tell me?"

Belinda reasoned, "Would you have listened? You know your grandparents love you and you didn't listen to them. Why would you listen to me? I thought it best to be your friend and be by your side so when the truth hit you would feel you had someone to talk to you. It must be true because you just told me things you haven't told anyone else."

Patty gave Belinda a hug, "You're right. I could have seen the truth for myself but didn't want to believe it. I never had a boyfriend. I never had a man make me feel special. Richard did that. I'm such a fool."

"No, you are not!" Belinda said in a very firm voice. "You are a good and beautiful person. You do lack a worldliness that would have made you realize the truth earlier. Your grandparents tried to protect you from negative people, but that took away your chance to learn to judge the good from the bad. You will meet the right person someday. You will find your Prince Charming."

Meanwhile, Jean was spending her time interviewing Barb. "Remember when we ran into Helen at the lawyer office that day? She said you recommended Mr. Craft. Can you tell me why? They have another lawyer they have used for years so why did she want to know the name of your attorney?"

Barb didn't mind answering Jean's questions. She understood they wanted to help her granddaughter even though she couldn't understand why this would help. "Helen asked about many parts of my life. Questions like where I shopped, who did my hair, what massage therapist I used. I found she started using a lot of the same people and saying I recommended for her to go to them. It was weird, like she wanted to come across as my best friend. The only reason we associated with them at all was because of Patty. Once we figured out what a horrible young man their son was, we cut off all invitations to visit our home. Regarding the lawyer, one night when Charles had gone on to bed, Helen said they planned to redo their wills and they didn't want to use their regular attorney because he was also Richard's attorney. Since most of the family business was open to Richard, she was worried their attorney would let it slip that they had work done on their wills. My husband and I could see that Charles has, let's call it, a mental problem. Sometimes he seems fine but other times he is very confused. I questioned if he could legally sign such a document but we didn't say a word. My husband gave her Mr. Craft's business card. I was surprised to see her leaving his office but not shocked. Mr. Craft thanked me for recommending my friend to use his service. She is not my friend. I try to act nice to everyone but not everyone is my friend."

Jean continued the tour of the home. She looked out on the patio and got a signal from Belinda that her interview was over so they went outside to watch a beautiful sunset together.

Chapter 35 – Team Meeting

The attack team had a meeting the next day to compare notes. Fannie reported, "Helen was nice to me, which is a red flag since she is only nice when she wants something. I did tell her I loved the coat and bought it for myself. She told me that since I dressed in a 1920s bathing suit, she wasn't surprised that I liked the 1920s style wool coat. I didn't know if that was an insult or not but acted like it was a compliment. Charles was resting and not to be disturbed. Helen said since Richard had died, Charles has become almost non-functioning due to grief but she was sure in time he would be fine."

Eve followed up on her end of the mission. "I don't have much to report. I was only permitted to use the guest bathroom on the main floor. There were only items a guest might need and no medications or anything of interest. Helen jumped up as soon as I came out and ushered me back to the formal front room so I didn't get to snoop. I did notice that there was mud on the side of Helen's car but she saw me looking so I bet it is gone now. I feel like I failed."

Fannie tried to comfort her, "No, you didn't fail. Helen is on full alert with us and made sure we were limited on what we saw. She also let us know, politely, that it was time to leave. There was nothing you could do about it."

Jean called her sister and put it on speaker, "I haven't gotten to talk to Priscilla yet. Mr. Thomas said he was with Priscilla as they completed the booking process. Priscilla promised not to say anything without Mr. Thomas in the room. They interviewed her but he kept telling her not to answer. They figured out that Priscilla wasn't going to be talking. I think her friendship with Nick kept them from being so hard on her. They didn't act tough but they tried to say they wanted her to tell everything so she wouldn't look guilty, and she might give them a clue to help free her. Mr. Thomas kept shaking his head no so Priscilla just stared at the floor and didn't answer. I see her walking into court now. She looks defeated. I need to get into court so she knows we are here with her and she is not alone."

Just then, Jean's phone rang. It was Alan. "Mom, it's important. Can you talk now?"

Jean answered, "We are reporting. Do you want to be on speaker or talk to me alone?"

Alan opted for the speaker, "I'm reporting in so speaker might be good. I talked to the boys a lot. They found out about their grandmother getting arrested. They are very upset and know she would never do that. It seems that Priscilla is the leak about the gun. Kathy told me that Priscilla would say anything funny she could think of to make the boys laugh. She told them the frog stories. She told them about Fannie's costume of the day and making a fool of herself around town. Sorry Fannie, if you're listening. No offense but really, an asp on your shoulder in a diner? She told them about how ridiculous some of the ladies acted when she found the gun. She told them it was real and demonstrated how she checked for bullets. They thought it was funny when Fannie liked the gun more after she found out its value. I asked if they repeated the story and they said yes. They said Helen is usually mean and short with them but after the gun story, she gave them cookies and kept asking questions but only about the gun story. I know that is important. Kathy told me about the stories last night. I'm with the boys now and just got the information from them about Helen being told. Do you think it would be ok to take the boys to Viking Heir with me? I got a lot of work and it isn't fair to put all the work on my wife."

Jean answered, "Sure, that's fine for the boys to go. It will be better than just sitting around the house waiting for word of their grandmother. Tell them we are getting the facts together and should have their grandmother cleared soon. Make sure to let Kathy know where they are. I'm assuming she is with Josephine, even though Josephine didn't say so when she reported."

"Yes, Kathy is at the courthouse. I will let them know." Alan signed off.

Belinda went next. "I interviewed Patty. She told me the whole story about what happened at the pub that night. She said Richard was standing on the path when she was trying to start the boat. But after the backfire, the boat started and she pulled away quickly. She never saw Richard again. I'm sure she didn't do it and things are exactly as she told me. I'm sure that her grandparents had nothing to do with it. Besides, we followed the clues and it only leads to Helen. She knew about the gun from the boys. She was here the day after the shooting and the gun was back after that. Even though we can't place her at the scene, anyone could have been there and hidden in the wooded area and not be seen. We need motive."

"Per Stirpes," said Jean.

"What is that?" asked Fannie.

Jean continued, "Charles would probably leave half his money to Helen and half to Richard, his wife and only son. If the Will said per stirpes and Richard were dead, then his half would go to Jerry and Craig. If it doesn't say per stirpes, then Helen inherits the whole thing. Remember at the pool party when Charles kept saying per stirpes was bad? I knew then that Helen got Charles to sign a Will cutting out the boys if Richard died before Charles. My friend, Vic, is their family and business attorney. He told me the ReSol family never went to any other attorney, which is why he was there for the divorce. I think Vic knows how bad Charles is with the dementia and he can't legally sign his name. I also think Vic would never believe that Charles would cut his grandsons out of the Will. Barb told me she thought Helen wanted the name of their attorney to imitate her. Being a friend of Barb's would make Helen more welcome and believable. Mr. Craft would not realize how bad the dementia was meeting Charles for the first time. When Helen was leaving his office, I recognized the folder was a standard type used to hold a Will. That is why Helen killed Richard. She is so greedy that she wanted it all."

Eve asked, "We know the truth, but how do we get the police to listen?"

Jean said, "Nick will believe us. He knows Priscilla too well to believe she is guilty. He is a good man and wouldn't let an innocent person go to jail."

Chapter 36 – Preparing for the Party

Jean called Nick, "Don't be mad, but we have been doing out own investigation and I think we have a good case that would free Priscilla."

Nick was amused. He said, "Don't be mad? It's what I expected you and your friends would do. I'm neither mad, nor surprised. I just heard that Josephine arranged the bail for Priscilla so they will be there soon. I'm working on my case right now and can't take a break. I'll be there tomorrow. We can talk after the murder mystery dinner party at Belinda's."

Jean was surprised, "I forgot all about the party. That will be fine. I miss you and can't wait to see you."

Fannie was making a gagging motion and Belinda looked up surprised, "I forgot about the party, too. I was so caught up in the investigation."

Eve asked, "Do you want to cancel? It would be understandable with all that is going on."

Belinda decided against the cancellation. "There are others invited and everything is ready. I took the box game and wrote other parts so everyone will have a person to act out. I just need to pick up the food. Fannie, can you help us all get costumes? It is a 1920's theme. I have my flapper dress at home but I don't know about the others."

Fannie did her magic and got everyone dressed in style. They stood in a group around a full size mirror. "Don't we look cute," said Eve.

Fannie dug out some spats and bowlers for the men to wear which she sent home with each of the ladies. "This is so much fun. No, put your purses away. You aren't going to pay the rental fee. Belinda can have more parties and invite people that will pay so I can earn some money."

Jean was calling Josephine to hear the news. "Yes, Priscilla is out. We are headed to her daughter's house now so she can take a long shower and get the jail germs off her. She doesn't want to come home because she is embarrassed and doesn't want to see anyone. She does say thank you to all of you. Thanks for believing in her and for working to free her. Can I tell her that progress has been made?"

Jean replied, "Yes, we are sure we have the story put together correctly and can push the police in the right direction. Nick promised to hear us out tomorrow night after the murder mystery party at Belinda's."

Jo was silent for a few seconds, "Seems like bad taste to have that type of party right now."

Jean defended the party, "Others not in our circle are invited. It would be in bad taste to cancel. Hopefully we can keep the conversation on that mystery and not our real life one. Do you need a costume?"

Jo said no, that she and Michael had their outfits already.

Eve continued to worry, "Do you really think Nick will believe us? I wish there was some way to prove Helen was there or didn't have an alibi."

Fannie said, "I asked her when and how they found out about Richard and she refused to talk about it. She said that if Charles overheard the conversation, it could make him worse re-living it. She told me never to bring up the topic to either of them again."

Chapter 37 – Investigating Miriam

Nick and Janice were on the way to Judith's apartment again. Mr. Cross wasn't really happy to see them. "I gave you her things and someone else has been in the apartment for over a month so I'm not letting you in there."

Janice came off more of a tiger than Nick so he let her take the lead, "I don't believe you gave us all her things. You said you gave the furniture to charity, but what did you do with her computer?"

Mr. Cross looked very sheepish, "Look, when a tenant leaves their things and they owe the landlord money, he has a right to sell the items to recover his loss of back rent. I'm within my legal right."

Janice growled, "You are obstructing a murder investigation. We want the computer. What else did you keep of hers?"

Mr. Cross produced a laptop. "She didn't have anything else of value. I have a few pieces of junk jewelry and the charger to a cell phone. That's it, really. I don't want you to take the computer because I started using it and my business stuff is on it."

Janice snatched the laptop, "It will be returned when we are finished, and if you object, I will arrest you for obstruction of justice. You knew we would need this and you lied."

Mr. Cross knew he was beaten, "I didn't lie. I just didn't tell you everything. I know I can't stop you but you have to give it back. I have my work matters backed up to a memory system so I don't have to have it anytime soon."

Janice was fuming when they got to the car, "That worm. He said he liked Judith but was too greedy to give us some help in catching her killer." Nick was laughing to himself but didn't dare laugh out loud. He loved to see his partner deflate men that thought they could push her around. She was one tough woman.

They were driving past the Visual Beauty warehouse and noticed Miriam's car in the lot. Miriam could see the officers in their car and remained hidden inside. She was relieved they didn't stop. It had been a few months now and at first she felt relief that Judith wasn't there to tell her scam. Only recently did she feel nervous. No one had said anything about the detectives since their visit but she felt like people looked at her differently. She felt like people weren't as friendly. She turned on the charm, "Art, you and Nora have outdone yourselves this time. The set will be perfect. I don't have a single criticism, only praise. Thank you for not just your excellent work on this set, but all the productions. I don't know what I would do without you." She gave them a hug goodbye and walked to her car.

Nora turned to her husband, "What the heck does she want? She always has something negative to say no matter how minor just to show she is the boss."

Art laughed, "I don't know or care. I'm just glad she is gone."

Miriam turned onto the road and was trying to think things through. The gun was a loose end. There was no way the police would connect her to the gun if it was back on the yacht. The blonde woman at the antique store may have recognized her. Snooping for the gun could create a connection. Miriam really believed that the police were stupid, and without that connection, they couldn't catch her. It had been odd for her lover to leave so abruptly but he said his wife made plans and he forgot. He would be gone the rest of the week, making it easier for her since she didn't have to justify being away from the yacht. Creighton thought he was such a great lover but the greatness was in her acting. Once she had enough money saved, she planned to leave him. She had the passwords to his computer and maybe could move some more money to her accounts without his knowing it. What a trusting fool he was. She once thought of killing his wife so she would become the grand lady but she didn't know if she could stand being with him that many more years. He thought he was using her but she was the one in control. Get blondie to give her the gun and then kill her and she would be home free.

Miriam returned to the yacht to collect a small suitcase loaded with what would be needed for a few nights just in case she needed to leave in an emergency. She armed herself with a pistol and a long range rifle. She moved all the bank balances to bank accounts that no one knew existed. She could move the money back if needed and no one would know the difference. She wished she knew how to get fake identification. She was too high up in life to know people like that but as an actor, she would figure out how to make herself into a lowlife and get that connection tonight. She wanted to be prepared for anything.

Chapter 38 – Discussing Cases

Nick couldn't wait to see Jean so he arrived that night around bedtime. Jean was so happy to see him. There was none of the tension that was present during their last visits. Jean didn't believe a couple should lie or keep secrets from each other. "Fannie told me about your getting in trouble at work. I really appreciate the tip about the same gun being used in both murders. I'm very glad you told me about the fingerprint location because it helped me figure things out. I know you said we would talk tomorrow after the party, but can we talk now so we can get it out of the way and enjoy tomorrow better?"

Nick held Jean close, "Good idea."

Jean spilled everything, "I know you said I was suspicious of Helen because I don't like her but here are the facts." Jean told him every detail the team had assembled.

Nick called Detective Ruiz and relayed those details. When he hung up, he smiled at Jean, "Great job. They have agreed to investigate those aspects of the case. You heard me tell them I didn't believe Priscilla did it, and they value my opinion. This doesn't put Priscilla in the clear. Don't you even tell the others because we don't want to tip off Helen and because everyone will get their hopes up that Priscilla will be freed. I'm so proud of you. Well played. I wish you could help on all my cases but that would be dangerous. If you promise not to tell I did it, I wouldn't mind talking out loud about my case. Just getting my thoughts in order, I'm not talking to you, understand?"

Jean laughed, "I'm just here writing and you're in the next room talking to yourself. Do you realize I haven't typed a single word since this all started? I'm so behind on my schedule."

Nick began repeating the steps of the investigation and ending with, "I just can't find the exact motive. Why kill Judith Lane? It can't be because she found out about the affair because everyone knows about it, including his wife. What a saint she is. The theatre group is on a break-even basis since it is a non-profit. Miriam is drawing a nice salary, not great but respectable. Living on the yacht, she has no expenses and can afford to dress in the style she likes. The accounting team can't find any difference in what she reports to the government and her books. What can she be doing that would cause her to commit murder?"

Jean had been typing on the computer. "The theatre group has an unusual name. If you look on Sunbiz, it is registered in the state of Florida as a not-for-profit corporation."

"So?" said Nick.

Jean liked having a trick up her sleeve, "Most companies incorporate in Delaware because of their tax laws. If you look on the Delaware corporate site, it shows a limited liability company registered under the same name. If you write checks to a company, you don't write out that part of the company name on the check. I bet if you check the banks, you will find Miriam Highland has an account open under the LLC at a different bank than the theatre uses. Checks like donations or grants could be deposited in either account without question. I bet Miriam is not reporting all the contributions the theatre has received to the Board of Directors."

"You are a genius," said Nick.

"There's more. I think Miriam is greedier than that. Do you think Mr. Creighton would give you the reports that Miriam provides to the Board of Directors?"

Nick nodded yes, "Mr. Creighton is done with Miriam. He is staying out of the way until we arrest her. Would that be a copy of the annual report shown to the public?"

Jean explained, "Yes, normally, but you said this is a rich man's tax write-off and they don't pay any attention to it, right? The missing seats make me think of a second con she could be pulling. You pay the theatre actors that are members of the union a salary based on the size of the theatre. The number of seats dictates the actor's paycheck. The number of seats also dictates the fees paid for the use of the play. The bigger the theatre, the more you pay the playwright. I would bet the seats that are removed are the ones paid for by the Creighton family. That is why she always wants to seat them. They sit somewhere other than their assigned seats. The Board of Directors thinks they have one size theatre when in reality they have a smaller one, since the size is determined by the number of seats and not the size of the building. You say the theatre is breaking even, but I would check to see if Miriam says they are losing money to the Board. I wonder if they are writing a check to the theatre to keep it operational? If they aren't, they wouldn't have a tax write-off."

Nick stared, "How do you know these things?"

"I am a writer, remember?" Jean acted offended.

Nick stammered, "But you write paperback murder mysteries."

Jean laughed, "Under one name. I also write plays and skits for churches under another name. What church would want to do a play by a murder writer? Josephine is a great musician. She's written several musicals. Unfortunately, none have ever made it big, but it is rewarding to have people see them even in a small town production. We keep following our dreams and someday we will both make it big. You need to keep believing someday your work will be appreciated. I waive my fee if a play or skit is performed in church. That is just my way to try to give back for the talent I was blessed with."

"I love you," said Nick.

"I love you, too," said Jean.

Chapter 39 – The Party

Belinda greeted her guests in full flapper style, a fringed dress, long strings of pearls, carrying a cigarette holder with a candy cigarette in the end and a feather in her hair. Steve walked up behind her in a pin-striped suit and a fedora on his head. "Better get in here, see. Things will be my way tonight, see."

Laughing, Nick asked, "Candy cigarette?"

The room was hopping. Belinda explained, "I created a CD with some of my favorites that will run about an hour. I love the music of the big band sound. We can Lindy Hop and Foxtrot all night. Don't you love the sounds of Louie Armstrong and Duke Ellington? I have some slower music by Bing Crosby and Bessie Smith mixed in because the Waltz was also big back then. I threw in some great Tango music too. Those were four of the five biggest dances at the time."

Right then, the perfect song for the Charleston came on and all four of them broke into the dance.

Steve suggested, "Let's go around the room and you say who you tried to dress like."

Fannie was obviously part of the woman's right to vote. She had a banner across her shoulder and a sign as she marched before the group. Michael tried to look like Rudolph Valentino and acted like the romantic lead. Fannie started chasing him with her sign shouting, "Women aren't objects." Alan imitated Charlie Chaplin because he likes his walking style, while his wife chose Felix the Cat. Each had their favorite from Clara Bow, Greta Garbo and Mary Pickford. The men incorporated the looks of Buster Keaton and Douglas Fairbanks but the mobsters and flappers were the favorites.

As Belinda passed out their roll cards, Eve asked Fannie, "Aren't you hot with that coat on? Aren't you going to take it off for dinner?"

"In real life, women marched outside so I need my coat on. This is the coat Helen hated and brought into the store. I love it," she explained.

The first course was served and wine was poured, "Let's pretend we are eating at a speakeasy," said Belinda. "I'm not sure I would have supported prohibition if I can't have wine with my meal."

They went around the table and each person read their character name and what they do. "I'm Lucy

Belle," said Fannie. "I love that name, and guess what I'm part of, the suffrage movement. Perfect!"

Jean read her card, "I'm a screen star." She batted her eyes and struck poses.

Around the table, the reading continued while they ate their salad. Soup was served as Belinda read who was killed. Everyone looked like they were eyeing the person next to them and you could hear them whisper things like "Did you do it?" "Don't kill me." "At least Felix has nine lives."

The soup was served and they started around the table to read their next statements. Fannie reached into her pocket but the card was missing. She took the coat off and found a slit in the pocket. "The card must have slipped into the lining. Wait, there's another paper there too. Give me a minute and I'll be right with you."

The others continued to read as Fannie pulled out the two papers and she froze. Steve asked, "Are you ready to read yours?"

Fannie turned to Jean and thrust the paper into her hand. It was a prescription for Haloperidol. "Do you know what this means?" she said emotionally. "This prescription is for Charles ReSol. This is not a drug you would use for someone with a milder case of dementia, only for more severe cases. That drug can have horrible side effects on some people. It can knock people out. Some people when taking this drug act like they are out of this world or can be down for days. I would never give it to Charles. He would be like a zombie. He wouldn't know what day it was or even what was happening around him. Remember how you said he acted at the funeral? That could be why."

"This isn't given unless the condition is very serious, right?" asked Jean. "Look at the date on the top. It was before the pool party."

Fannie turned to Nick, "Someone needs to check on that man. I doubt if she is giving him the best care."

Nick assured Fannie, "I will look into it. Don't worry. I understand how serious you think this is."

They tried to resume the party but it was without the fun and heart that was there before.

Fannie apologized to everyone and felt bad for ruining the party.

Belinda assured her friend, "You didn't ruin it. Helen did."

Chapter 40 – The Farmhouse Auction

The next day, Nick was up early and off to work.

Jo and Michael agreed to watch the store. Jean was going with Fannie to an auction at a farm located in the back woods. "Fannie, don't worry. Nick is on both cases now. He will check on Charles." Jean was also worried that Miriam Highland wasn't through, but didn't tease Fannie about babysitting her. Fannie was not in a mood to be teased. True to her word, she never mentioned Nick's investigation but she was worried about both Helen and Miriam because when the trap was about to fall, the killer would be like wild animals and be in their most dangerous frame of mind. She wished she had a gun even though she really disliked them. Jean was trying to keep a look out but didn't see two cars watching as they pulled away from the store.

Miriam watched as her victim pulled out. She had the guns but a car accident would be preferable. She watched as Fannie took the Wyatt Earp style outfit out of the front window and boxed it up. Fannie also took the guns out of the drawer from behind the counter. She then carried the box to the car. Maybe the real gun would be there this time, she hoped.

Another car was in the back alley. Helen watched as Fannie put on her wool coat. Helen remembered that she was wearing that coat when she got her husband's prescription. She wanted it back because she didn't want proof existing that her husband was on dementia medicine before the Will was signed. She altered the date on the doctor's chart when he left the room but there was still a lot of evidence of his condition. She was trying to cover what she could. She thought about asking for the coat back, saying something like, 'He noticed I wasn't wearing it and I told him it was at the cleaners.' Helen knew Fannie didn't like her, no matter how friendly she acted on the last visit. She might not give it back out of meanness.

Jean kept looking in the rearview mirror as they drove. "I noticed a blue sedan has been on our tail for a while. It's too far back and I can't see who is driving it."

Fannie dismissed her friend's worries, "This is a back road with very few streets that run off of it. If someone is behind us, where else could they turn off? They would have to stay behind us until the next town."

Fannie slowed to turn down a dirt road. "What on earth could someone living way out here have that you would want?" Jean was edgy as she asked.

Fannie laughed, "Back here is where they have the true antiques. I bet we get a lot of great treasure today."

The blue sedan went straight ahead so Jean felt a little better about it.

Jean came out of her funk as Fannie registered for bidding. The old farm house was good size, white with two stories. Maybe her friend was right that it might be full of antiques. A loud gunshot was heard and Fannie and Jean both jumped. The auctioneer laughed at them. "It's hunting season. We will be hearing that noise all day long. Don't worry, there are rules on hunting and they won't be firing this way."

The day was warm so Fannie took off her coat and put it on the driver's seat of the car. "I thought you even slept in that thing. It's been hot and you have had it on all the time anyway," Jean observed.

Fannie just shot an annoyed look at her friend. The box with the Wyatt Earp costume came out, "When the owner of the house came to town to advertise his auction, he saw the outfit and loved it. He's a good old country boy with a romantic view of the past. He really gave me a good price for it. It was a good draw to the store but I can't pass up the money."

The auctioneer suggested the bidders walk through the house. Everything that was not going to be auctioned was in the parlor to the right of the front door so the bidders weren't to go in there. Everything else would be brought out and sold. "You might want to see what is available so you hold back funds for the treasure to come out later."

Fannie and Jean entered the house. Fannie was in heaven. There were steamer trunks and a hope chest. The kitchen had two antique wooden cabinets with glass fronts that were used to store canned goods and dishes. There weren't any cabinets on the walls or closets in the bedroom but there were a few armoires. There was a hall tree and umbrella stand. There was an iron stand that you placed the heel of your boot in to help remove them.

Fannie said so excited, "I want it all. There is so much here, we might have to stay late to get the best prices. I will bid when the price is right and stay until I'm out of money. You will have to accept my time schedule and not complain since you insisted on coming with me."

They climbed into the attic where they found a baby cradle, clothing, old newspapers from the 1800's and more. Looking out the attic window, Jean admitted, "We are really out in the country. Just look outside and see how beautiful it is. You can see for miles without a power line or phone line unless you're looking towards the road. It's almost like stepping back in time. It's even a little romantic. If I saw a guy in a western outfit walking by, I would think we stepped back in time. WHAT THE ___"

Fannie turned, "What's wrong with you?"

Jean pointed down and shouted, "Look!"

Fannie saw Helen opening the door of the van and reaching in to get the coat. A shot rang out and Helen fell forward. The crowd at the auction ducked down except three men that ran towards Helen. The auctioneer was shouting, "Fannie!"

Jean was on the phone to Nick who assured her, "Police and an ambulance are on the way. We are at the road where it turns into the dirt trail. I can see Miriam's car pulled off into a group of trees. Get Fannie inside and both of you stay there until I arrive."

Jean for once did just what she was told. The owner was standing nearby. She told him quickly about the situation and he ordered all the people to either go into the house or the barns until he gave an all clear. Jean pushed Fannie inside and away from the windows.

Both sat quietly and in shock.

Chapter 41 – Fannie's Lament

Nick and Janice both rushed into the house and threw their arms around Fannie and Jean. The four stood and held tight for the longest time. Nick whispered, "That could have been either one of you that was shot instead of Helen. Miriam thought it was Fannie because with Helen's back towards her and getting into Fannie's van, she thought she killed Fannie."

Janice warned, "That's why you shouldn't investigate. It scares me to think Fannie might have been killed."

Jean answered with her logic, "Well, if we didn't investigate, it could have been Fannie that was shot. Thanks to our investigation, Helen was here to take the bullet for us. That was a good thing, right?"

Nick laughed, "You do have your own way of looking at things."

Jean wanted to know, "The blue sedan that was following us. Was that Helen or Miriam?"

"Helen," said Nick, "I'm glad to know you observed that at least. I don't believe Miriam realized how much we had on her. She wanted to get the gun back and get Fannie out of the way so she wouldn't tell of her trip to the Attic trying to get the gun. Thanks to you, Jean, we had the case wrapped up and were trying to locate her for the arrest. We had an APB on her car. Driving a Mercedes in this back country stuck out like a sore thumb, and the sheriff called us immediately. I just asked if there was an auction nearby and knew this was where everyone was headed."

Fannie asked, "Is Helen dead? Oh my gosh, I just realized the person was trying to kill me. Helen looked like me from behind. Helen was in my van." The others had to help Fannie to a seat as her knees started to buckle.

Jean hugged her friend, "It's ok now. Look on the bright side."

"BRIGHT SIDE?" yelled Fannie.

"No more Fannie-sitting. You won't have us hanging around the store all day," said Jean.

Fannie glared, "I hate the term Fannie-sitting." In a nicer voice, she said, "I will actually miss all the friends hanging around, a little anyway."

Jean asked, "Do you want us to keep up our shifts?"

Fannie laughed, "I won't miss you that much." Everyone joined in the laugh.

Fannie asked, "Gross, a dead body in my van. Do you think the insurance company will buy me a new one?"

Nick shook his head no, "I don't think that will work. In fact, more good news is the van didn't even get a scratch because Miriam was a great shot. There is a little blood but I'll make sure the van is cleaned before we return it to you. While it is a crime scene now, since there were so many witnesses, we won't have it long."

"That's your good news. It is gross. I might have to buy a new one. I'll have nightmares when I'm around it," moaned Fannie.

Chapter 42

On the front porch of the Home, Jean, Josephine, Eve, Belinda and Priscilla sat, rocking and drinking lemonades. Eve said, "Do you realize how many hours we have spent here listening to Jean's murder mysteries? Who would even believe we would actually be a part of one?"

Priscilla shivered, "I don't want to hear a story, even a fictional one, for a long time. That was the most horrible experience of my life. I still have nightmares. I can guarantee I will never wish someone was dead again."

Jean asked, "How are the boys and Kathy doing?"

Priscilla answered, "Kathy is fine. Financially, she is better because she gets social security for the boys now. They will also get some help for college. The boys both have nightmares but a phycologist we know is offering free service to them. I think I need one too because I admit to nightmares. You won't believe the good news. Charles is no longer on the medication too strong for him and while he still has some memory issues, he seems normal most days. He is spending a lot of time with Kathy and the boys. Charles asked that Kathy be appointed guardian and the court approved it. The boys will inherit everything. Kathy will get paid a small fee for the care she gives him. For now, Kathy and the boys can't receive much of the money because the funds are needed for the care Charles receives, but chances are good there will be plenty left for my grandsons to have a bright future."

Josephine agreed, "It takes time to get over something like this but everything is going to be ok."

Priscilla was emotional when she said, "I know I've thanked you all a million times. Let's make it a million and one. Thank you all so much for supporting me, for doing the investigation, for being there with my daughter and grandsons. I can't tell you how grateful I was to look up and see you, Josephine, in the court room. For all of you putting up the bail money so I didn't have to spend another night in fear in that jail cell. You are the best friends in the world." Tears started to flow once more.

Jean was reflecting on the events, "It all comes down to one word: greed. Miriam was greedy for more money. Helen would have inherited a huge fortune with just getting half of Charles' estate but had to have more. Greed caused Richard to leave his family and wanting to marry for money. In reality, they all threw away their lives and ended up with nothing. Even if Richard and Helen had lived, they would have had nothing. I will never understand people being selfish and hateful. I'm choosing to live here, even though I can afford a more expensive place, because the closeness I feel to my grandfather and great grandfather. I don't care about being rich and famous. Ok, maybe I'll go for the rich but not at the expense of someone else."

Josephine looked at the time, "We better head down the street for tea at Fannie's so we can hear Fannie and Jean do their usual 'I don't sell tea fight.' It is so good to be back to normal. Hey Belinda, let's have another mystery dinner party soon. Let's do a Wild West theme and I get to be the madam of a brothel."

"Count me out," said Priscilla.

They all laughed and walked arm-in-arm to Fannie Annie's Attic.

Mia Tenroc

ABOUT THE AUTHOR

Mia Tenroc started reading mysteries when she was 12 years old, Rex Stout and Agatha Christie being her favorites. She and her sister vowed to become mystery writers. Unable to work together, Mia designed the series with central characters that introduce each story in the first chapter but then each book is its own story. That way, she and her sister could write their own stories yet use these characters as the connection.

Mia's books are dedicated to demonstrating how what we say to one another really matters. She hopes to show that kind words build self-esteem and elevates people. A dedicated people watcher, Mia observes families interacting with each other which she uses as the basis for her books.

Mia tries to incorporate her small town into the books because there is a great joy in knowing your neighbors and being surrounded by family and friends. Mia loves to travel and experience the fun of seeing new place.

ORDERING INFORMATION

To get copies of this and other books by Mia Tenroc, please contact:

McToner Publishing Inc.
P.O. Box 37
Goldenrod, Florida 32722
McTonerPublishing@gmail.com
www.Miatenroc.com

Also available on many online book sellers.